Everything's
FINE

Everything's
FINE

JANCI PATTERSON

GARDEN
NINJA
BOOKS

Edited by Kristina Kugler
Cover Design by Melody Fender

Published by Garden Ninja Books

JanciPatterson.com

First Edition: June 2014

0 9 8 7 6 5 4 3 2 1

For Kristy—
I love you
Fifty million billion—

And for Melody—
Who knows just how complicated
High school friendships can be.
Love you.

Without the hard work of these two,
You wouldn't be holding this book.

Hindsight

Everyone wants to know what happened to Haylee. One day she was here, and the next she wasn't. It's easy to blame me. I was her best friend. I should have seen this coming. And I get that. Believe me, I do.

But here's the thing you have to understand. Haylee never used the word suicide. She never told me she wanted to die. Not once.

Except.

There was one thing she used to say, when things were getting better. After the days of hiding her face, she'd throw her arms open to the sky and spin round and round, like she'd just discovered the world and wanted to drink it all in.

She'd turn to me, then, her face glowing, and ask: "Will you miss me, when I make my exit?"

I thought she was talking about running away. She'd told me the story over and over, each time a little different. She was going to hitchhike down to LA and sleep with whichever directors she had to. When she was a famous movie star who got paid millions per picture, she'd retire to the stage, which was her one true love.

"I'll come with you," I used to tell her. "You'll need a manager." Even though what did I know about Hollywood? Nothing. And Haylee always gave me this sad look, which I thought meant she knew we'd never go. It's the only clue Haylee gave me, the only road sign for what was coming. So tell me, would you have understood what she meant? Would you have been able to stop her?

There was one more thing, three months ago. I'd walked over during the first rainstorm of fall. It was only sprinkling when I left my house, but in four short blocks, the rain pounded down on me, and I jogged the rest of the way with my hood stretched tight over my face, drawstring drawn, so that only my eyes and nose poked out. Haylee's mom let me in, and I shed my sopping hoodie in their entryway and pounded up the stairs in my squelching sneakers.

I knocked on Haylee's door, and when she didn't answer, I opened it.

I can still see her standing in front of the window of her room, screen cast aside on the floor, stretching her arms out, catching the thick drops of rain as they plunged out of her tree. She wore a pair of tight black leggings and a loose, gauzy pink shirt that blew backward in the wind, entangled in her lace curtains. Her long, blond hair was divided into two spiral braids that twisted down her back. She spun around, holding her wet arms out for me to see, and her braids hit the window frame with two smacks.

I stood in her doorway, unsure if I should step in or out. Hurricane Haylee could blow stronger than the wind, pound harder than the rain, and I couldn't tell if it was coming or going.

But she smiled, though her eyes and cheeks were as red and puffy as the new scratches on her arms, though the old ones had faded to scattered shades of pink and white.

I knew where she got those. Everyone knew about that.

She turned her wet wrists so droplets drizzled onto the white carpet.

One of them was tinged pink.

"Amazing," Haylee said. She turned back to the window, watching the branches outside bowing in the wind. "I'm going to miss this."

And like an idiot, I thought she was talking about the tree.

One Week After

My mom drove us from the church to the graveyard on the day of Haylee's funeral. I'd never noticed how many crumbs had embedded themselves into the carpet of the car, and I tried to identify them one by one. The half of the pretzel was easy. A chunk of the white crumbs was still shaped like the ridged edge of a saltine. Some dark, runny substance had glued itself to the edge of the carpet just below the weather stripping. I was almost glad I couldn't tell what that was.

A Christmas wreath hung on the automatic gate. If I'd stretched my arms wide, I don't think I could have touched both edges of it, and the bow at the bottom was bigger than some of the dresses I'd seen at school dances. Mom inched the car forward as the gate crawled open.

"Are you okay?" Mom asked.

"Sure," I said. "Peachy." Any other day, Mom would have told me to stop being snotty. This time she just stared out the window, letting it slide. Apparently even my school psychologist mother couldn't find words for today.

A crowd had beat us to the graveside. Mom parked down the little stone drive and I climbed out. The air was cold enough to show my breath, and I huddled down inside my jacket and tried not to breathe, because Haylee wasn't breathing, and her body wasn't warm enough to turn the air into steam, and it would never do that again. I pinched my arm, because that was a stupid thing to be thinking; who, on the day of their funeral, would actually miss the way their breath clouded up in the air?

Haylee. That's who.

And then we were standing at the back of the crowd of people, though I didn't remember entirely how I'd gotten there.

A minister spoke at the grave—the same one who'd spoken at the funeral. He had pasty skin rimmed by five o'clock shadow, and I don't remember a single word he said, only that he talked as if he knew Haylee, when I was positive that her family had never gone to church. He'd been given those words to say, a total stranger speaking like he'd been Haylee's friend, while the rest of us stood silently on.

And then the minister's voice was still, and I looked up from the lint spot on the coat of the person in front of me, and I found a line forming. The casket had already been lowered into the grave, and everyone filed by, throwing in their handful of dirt. My mother nudged me forward, but my knees locked. My new black heels sank slowly into the mud.

Mom stepped around me and joined the line, and I stood alone while the others behind us did the same. A shadow spread over me, shielding me entirely from the sun. I looked up to find Haylee's cousin Nick standing over me. Nick was a junior at my school—a year and a half older than Haylee and me. He was a good foot taller than I was, and he had the same sandy-blond hair as Haylee, only his always hung in his eyes. He wore a white collared shirt and a tie. I'd never seen him wear anything but a T-shirt in all the years I'd known him.

"Hey," he said.

"Hey," I said back.

And I searched for something to say that didn't sound stupid or false, but my breath just kept sliding in and out of my lungs and I couldn't help but think, without Haylee to fish words out of me, would I ever speak to anyone again?

His fingertips brushed mine, and I thought for a moment that he was going to take my hand and lead me to the line, and if he had I would have let him, because even today I wouldn't be able to let go of Nick Harbourne's hand if it was finally—miraculously—holding mine.

But instead he put a hand on my shoulder, soft and tentative, and squeezed it once. Then he stepped around me and joined the line.

And when I looked up to watch him, my eyes met Haylee's father's across the grave.

Aaron was my pitching coach, and my softball sponsor. We spent almost as much time together as I spent with Haylee, and more time together than he spent with her. If he noticed he was staring at me, he didn't react. He held my gaze, his face entirely blank. Shadows darkened his cheeks, and his eyes looked like they'd physically sunk back into his head. When he looked at me, I wondered if he saw all those hours he should have been spending with her. I wondered if he regretted it, now.

If he'd made a different choice, would we be standing here at all?

People pressed around me again. The line had wrapped around behind me, so I now stood near the front of the group instead of the back. Mom came and stood directly beside me, so close that her sleeve pressed against mine. I looked down at our feet, close together in the mud. I waited, to see if Nick would come back, but he must have gone somewhere behind me. I thought about turning to look, but my neck stayed frozen in place.

Only Aaron and I didn't toss any dirt. As the last of the line shuffled by, he stared down into the hole that had swallowed his daughter.

I wanted to tell him that Haylee wasn't in the ground, not really. She was gone days before, when she climbed out of her skin and wandered away. Tossing her into the hole was only a ritual. A distraction from the cold, hard truth.

Shut in her bedroom, Haylee finally made her exit.

And she left me here. Alone.

11

Chapter One

At the reception after Haylee's funeral, I stood in the corner of Haylee's kitchen, wedged between the pantry door and the corner of the refrigerator, slurping Jell-O. Something about Jell-O's texture bothers me, the way you can't drink it, but you can't chew it, either. But Haylee's aunt had handed me a plateful of it, so I poked at it until I caught Nick's younger sister staring at me. Then I shoveled a sporkful into my mouth.

People filled Haylee's house, standing in the halls, sitting on couch arms and in fold-up chairs. I wondered what they would have been doing on a Sunday afternoon if they weren't here. They'd all come with only a few days notice. Friends had canceled plans; family had flown in from out of town. Mom displaced her grocery shopping; Haylee's mom canceled her weekly massage. If you'd asked me a week ago what I'd be doing today, I would have told you I'd be lounging on Haylee's bed, eating peach rings and making excuses not to go home.

When I'd finished all the Jell-O I could manage, I dragged the tines across the Styrofoam, raking little lines like the ones on Haylee's arms. Regardless of where we had meant to be, here we were, in an after-school special. This week, Kira loses her best friend. Tune in to see how she copes.

If this was the end of a movie, I'd give it failing marks for foreshadowing. Haylee knew everything about me—every fight I'd had with my mother, every reason I wished I was born into her family instead of mine. She knew every word Nick had spoken to me over the last seven years, every time he touched me, or nearly did, or just plain didn't. I didn't have to worry about her judging me; however crazy I was, Haylee was always crazier. I knew everything about her, and she knew everything about me, and we still liked each other, which was the real miracle.

But here I was, in a sea of people asking why, with no better answers than they had.

I tilted my plate, letting what remained of my Jell-O slide along the lip of my plate, trying to decide what I would put on the chemistry test if Mr. Ivers asked if it was a liquid or a solid. I'd probably put down solquid, and hope for partial credit.

I had my mouth full of solquid when Haylee's mom, Hazel, came up and put her arm around me. Her skin was pale, but she had on bright lipstick so she looked like Snow White, or maybe Snow White's mother. She had to press her butt against the refrigerator to stand that close to me, and a magnet Haylee had painted in fifth grade fell to the floor. It smiled up at me—a wooden sunshine wearing huge sunglasses.

"Thank you for coming," Hazel said to me. I'd heard her say that to fifteen people, at least. She had her mantra; I had my Jell-O.

"Where's Aaron?" I asked.

"I think he went upstairs for a minute," she said. "He's taking this hard."

That seemed like a stupid thing to say. Their daughter had died. How else was he supposed to take it? But I hadn't heard anyone say a helpful thing yet, so maybe stupid words were our only options. For my part, I chose the least stupid words I could think of.

"I miss her," I said. I'd gone more than a week without talking to her before. But I couldn't remember a time when I *couldn't* call her.

Hazel squeezed her arm around my waist. "I know you do," she said.

"I'm sorry," I said. Everyone seemed to be saying that, but it was true. There were so many things to be sorry for.

Hazel hesitated, chewing on her lip in the same way Haylee did—the way that meant she wanted to say something difficult, but didn't know how.

Hazel's lips were the same shape as Haylee's—full and soft—only Hazel's had sharp wrinkles at the corners of her mouth, from frowning, not from smiling. If she'd been Haylee, I would have badgered it out of her. *Come on*, I'd say. *You know you're going to spill it eventually.*

But Hazel wasn't Haylee.

I waited.

Hazel's arm squeezed me tighter, like a boa constrictor. "I've been looking for Haylee's journal," she said. "You know, the one her therapist asked her to keep."

The journal. With those things that Haylee wrote about me.

My hands went cold, and I disentangled myself from her and dropped my plate in the garbage, watching the Jell-O slide onto the black plastic bag.

"I don't know where it is," I said.

I half expected her to call me on the lie. Of course I knew where it was. I knew everything about Haylee.

Except we were standing in the middle of the evidence that I didn't.

"I'm only trying to understand what happened," she said. "If you have any idea where she kept it—"

"I don't," I said. "I'm sorry."

Then I looked Hazel in the eye for the first time that day. Under her makeup her eyelids were puffy. She looked like she had more wrinkles than usual, and her skin had gone gray. I hated myself for not helping her, but this was the way it had to be.

I'd never kept a journal. I couldn't be honest in one and then leave it lying around for Mom to nose through. Besides, I had

Haylee. But Haylee's shrink made her keep one. Write down everything, she said. You can sort out what's important later.

I didn't want anyone reading the things I told to Haylee. But worse—far worse—were the things that weren't true, the ones that existed only in Haylee's mind. It wasn't her fault, really. She had a knack for telling lies and then believing them. Once she did, no one could talk her out of them. Not even me. Usually the lies were about herself. She got a B on a pop quiz; obviously she was stupid. She got picked last for volleyball when I got picked first; obviously everyone hated her. Her dad spent an afternoon helping me perfect my dropball; obviously he didn't love her.

But sometimes. Sometimes the lies she made up were about me. And if someone read those, they'd have no way to sort the truth from the lies. There was a sort of a weight to words that were written down—it was so much easier to believe them. Haylee's therapist, her mother, *my* mother . . . they'd think every word was true.

Hazel was still talking. "If you remember anything," she said, "even if it's just an idea, please let me know."

"Okay," I said. The journal was hidden, but not *that* well. They'd have to clean out Haylee's room. They'd find it eventually. "I need to go to the bathroom." I turned and pushed my way to the hall, and Hazel didn't stop me.

The downstairs bathroom was occupied, which gave me the perfect excuse to sneak upstairs. Frames lined the hallway, filled with pictures of Haylee and her cousins. I stopped in front of a photo of the two of us outside a theater in San Francisco—the only picture of me in the hall. We were wearing these matching skirts that were stupidly short, but it was okay because we were nine years old with twiggy thighs and no hips. Haylee hit puberty the next year. It took me another four years to catch up in the hip department, and to this day I was flat as could be.

I paused outside the upstairs bathroom. I could just use it like I said I would, and go back downstairs. If Hazel didn't know where the journal was, it might take her a while to find it.

15

But she *would* find it eventually. And I couldn't risk the questions that would follow.

I pushed open the door to Haylee's room, which was shut but not locked. The room seemed like it was holding its breath, waiting for her to return. Old play programs littered her desk from the shows we'd gone to last summer at the classical Greek theater in Santa Cruz. On top of them lay a clean, printed copy of Haylee's essay on *Tess of the D'Urbervilles*, the one that was due before Christmas break.

Her purple bedspread lay smooth across her sheets, tucked in at the edges. That was wrong. I shut the door behind me and tugged on the blanket, wadding it up and stuffing it at the end of the bed, the way Haylee would have left it.

It smelled of detergent, and that was wrong, too. Hazel had washed the bedding. Everything else in Hazel's house was always newly-laundered, but Haylee made a stand for her room. It should be messy, just like her mind.

Besides, who washed their dead daughter's bedding days after she died?

I froze. Was that where her body had been? I stood with both feet planted on the floor, and imagined slipping out of my body and drifting away. What happened to her body, once Haylee was gone? Did it go limp, or stiff? Did her spirit escape, or was she trapped inside as we locked her in cold storage, put her on display, and then dumped her in the ground?

Mom wouldn't tell me how Haylee did it. I was sure Haylee's death would be in the news, but the only thing I could find online was an obituary. I guess a teen suicide wasn't a big enough deal to be reported. One day Haylee was there, the next she was gone. Not much of a story, really. That meant I knew nothing except what my mother would tell me. And she was too busy reading books about how to help your teen through a death to notice me.

I didn't know much about killing yourself, but I couldn't imagine it was easy. Maybe if you had a gun, but Haylee's parents weren't gun people. When we were little, her mom wouldn't even let us play with squirt guns, unless they were the useless kind shaped like spitting frogs or dolphins instead of firearms.

If Haylee died a bloody death in her bed, the bedding wouldn't have washed easily, if at all.

My stomach turned.

Don't think. Get the journal.

I opened the closet. It looked even more a wreck than usual. Hazel must have been in here, looking. Or maybe Haylee had torn it apart in her last minutes, consumed by one of her fits, blind to everything but her pain. Once, years ago, I'd watched her destroy her math textbook, tearing and tearing until no page was left intact.

"I don't get it," she said. "I just don't get it."

I should have realized then she wasn't talking about math.

At the bottom of the closet, sparkles shimmered. I pulled out Haylee's Winter Fling dress, smoothing out the wrinkles in the black fabric. Silver glitter dusted the floor.

Last time I'd seen Haylee, she'd modeled the dress for me at the store before she bought it. The top fit tight, straps criss-crossing over her shoulder blades. The skirt cascaded over her hips and billowed out, so it swished when she turned, just wide enough to be classy, just tight enough to be sexy. Her hands ran over the skirt like each thread was precious. Haylee had worn that dress to go out with Bradley Johansen. The one, true Bradley Johansen. And then she'd never called me again.

I'd tried to call him the day I found out about Haylee. I'd called twice more since then, but he hadn't answered. I was sure that I'd see him at school, or at the funeral. But I'd skipped school on Monday, and he'd been out the rest of the week. I hadn't seen him at the service, or the burial, or the reception.

He *should* be here—if he liked her enough to take her to the dance, he should care enough to suffer along with the rest of us.

Focus, I told myself, hanging Haylee's dress over an open dresser drawer. He had to come back to school eventually. For now, I had to deal with the journal.

I lifted the shoe rack that had been below the dress. Beneath it, the carpet lay loose against the wall. I reached under it; my fingers met paper and I pulled.

The journal slid free. I held it tight. The front cover had a picture of a willow tree, and a quote from William Shakespeare:

All the world's a stage,
And all the men and women merely players:
They have their exits and their entrances;
And one man in his time plays many parts,
His acts being seven ages.

I wanted to take a permanent marker over the third line, especially that word: exit.

Stairs creaked at the end of the hallway. Footsteps drew closer. I stepped behind the closet door, holding absolutely still, squeezing shut the pages of the journal in my hand. If Hazel came in now, where would I stash the journal? I wouldn't be able to jam it back beneath the carpet in time, and I hadn't brought a purse.

The feet paused outside Haylee's door. My heart pounded as the seconds ticked by. Had my breathing always been this noisy? I tried to take shallower breaths, but my lungs began to ache, demanding more air.

Then the door to the bathroom clicked closed, and I heard the sound of the toilet cover being lifted. From the volume of the sound of urine hitting the toilet, the person had to be standing up.

I couldn't move, for fear it was someone else inclined to investigate, but at least if it was a man, it wasn't Hazel.

I let out a long breath and took another one in, trying to calm my heart. My fingers twitched over a bent corner of a journal page. Mom said there'd been no suicide note, but certainly this is where it would be—Haylee's last words, where only I could find them.

I flipped the book open, sifting quietly through the blank

pages at the back.

The toilet flushed across the hall, and I heard the bathroom door open again just as I came to the last written page. There was no date, only a single sentence: *The stairs creak in the night, and interrupt my dreams.*

What kind of a note was that? That could have been written anytime—even before the dance.

The footsteps came back into the hall, and I waited, holding my breath, for them to walk back down the stairs. But they paused outside Haylee's door again. Waiting.

In all likelihood, listening.

There was no more time for reading now. I couldn't get caught with the journal in my hands—not when I'd just lied about it. Shoving it under the carpet would take too long, and make too much noise. I leaned toward the window. Could I drop it out into the bushes below?

But the blinds behind the curtains would clank, and the sound of the window dragging open would be unmistakable. Plus, the house was crawling with people, new guests arriving all the time. Someone would see.

The hallway was silent. Had whoever it was wandered away? I moved slowly to Haylee's door, easing each footfall onto the carpet. I turned the lock on Haylee's door, slowly, quietly.

I still couldn't read the journal here. If someone found the door locked, they might knock. I couldn't exactly cower in here. Hazel would know instantly what I'd been doing. What I needed was a place to hide the journal—somewhere Hazel wouldn't immediately look.

My eyes settled on the crawlspace—a hatch in the closet ceiling that led to a space under the roof, filled with insulation.

Another floorboard creaked in the hall, and I made a split-second decision. I grabbed Haylee's chair from her desk, lifting it as quietly as I could and setting the legs down on the clothes in the bottom of the closet. I stepped up onto the chair and reached for the crawlspace, pushing the hatch door up a few inches and shoving the journal underneath the layers of insulation.

Dust drifted down into my eyes, and I fought the urge to sneeze. I took an involuntary sharp breath, and dropped both my hands to plug my nose and cover my mouth.

The hatch banged back into place.

I cringed, and my whole body hunched. If someone was in the hall, they'd definitely heard.

A heartbeat later, Haylee's doorknob rattled.

Seventeen Months Before

Haylee's family had a party every year on the fourth of July. Hazel invited all the neighbors, all Aaron's friends from work, and Haylee's entire extended family.

During the party, Haylee's backyard fizzed with soda, streamers, and sparklers. Hazel covered the roof in blankets so people could climb up and watch when the fireworks started. She cleaned the house, groomed the yard, and spread out so much food there wasn't room for it on the ten-foot table.

This year, Aaron tried to draft me into a night game of touch football with the neighborhood boys. They played with a glowing Nerf ball and hung glowstick bracelets from every ankle and wrist—from a distance, the game looked like a battle between awkward, oversized fireflies.

Playing football with boys in the dark sounded like a good way to get groped by twelve year olds. "I'm not really a football person," I told Aaron.

"Eh," he said. "You're in better shape than any of them. Faster, too."

I hesitated. "Is Nick playing?"

Aaron shrugged. "I tried to convince him, but he said the same thing you did."

I smiled. Nick wasn't one to play any sport, but I could still be happy we had this in common.

"See if you can convince him," Aaron said. "Bring Haylee, if you can find her."

I couldn't. She'd disappeared to refill the chip bowl, and never returned. Haylee was nowhere—not in the yard, not in the house, not even in her room, where Nick's younger sister and her friends had gathered to watch a movie on someone's laptop.

I returned to the yard and found Nick sitting on a lounge chair in one corner, watching as his brothers chased each other in circles, sparklers in hand. The football game might be a good excuse to touch him, but what I really wanted was to sit by him and talk. I wasn't brave enough to plop down next to him. Instead, I casually walked by four different times, waiting for Nick to invite me to sit.

He smiled at me twice, and my skin tingled. But each time he turned back to his brothers.

Four times was already bordering on stalking; five would be ludicrous. And if I sat down next to him now, it would be obvious I'd been pacing back and forth, trying to work up the nerve. So I went back to searching for Haylee.

I don't know what set her off. It might have been the sparklers. They're illegal in our county. No one was going to call the cops— one of the neighbors was a police officer, and he had one in his own hand. But I finally found her shut in the pantry, chewing on a fruit roll-up. She fidgeted against the shelves, like a cornered mouse.

"Can we get out of here?" she asked.

"Your dad wants us to play football," I said.

Haylee gave me a dark look. The football game was a trifecta of things Haylee avoided—sports, crowds, and her father. "Can't we just go for a walk?" she asked.

The sky had already settled into true darkness, so Hazel wouldn't appreciate that, and neither of us were old enough to drive. Nick had just gotten his learner's permit a few months ago, so he wasn't supposed to drive without a licensed adult.

But I remembered the cop with the sparkler. This was a night for breaking rules.

"Hang on," I said, and I shut Haylee back in the pantry.

Nick was still sitting alone on his chair. He wasn't much for parties either, but instead of hiding away like Haylee, he sat on the sidelines and watched.

Now that I had a real reason to talk to him, I marched right up and tugged on his sleeve. "Haylee needs to get out of here," I said. "Can we go for a ride?"

Nick shook his head. "Her mom would be ticked."

That was true. Nick's mom and Hazel were sisters, but Nick's mom was pretty relaxed, while Hazel was totally anal. "But Haylee really needs this. Just for half an hour. Maybe Hazel won't notice."

Nick chewed his lip for a moment. "I'll think of an excuse," he said.

I grinned. "We'll meet you at your car."

Haylee and I slunk through the house, taking the side door through the garage and out to the street. One of the families down the road was setting off rockets in the street, but Nick had left his car unlocked, so I ushered Haylee inside and rolled up his windows. She curled up on the back seat, her forehead pressed to her knees.

Nick opened the driver's side door a few minutes later. He winked at me. "I can't believe Aunt Hazel ran out of paper plates," he said. "Guess we'll have to go get some more."

I'd seen the mountain of paper goods Hazel bought for the party. "Where'd you hide them?" I asked.

"In the trunk of her car."

I laughed. She'd find them later, and blame her scattered brain. I sat in the passenger seat as Nick drove to the convenience store down the street. Every patch of grass along the side of the road was papered with blankets and bodies, everyone lounging and waiting for the fireworks.

By the time we pulled into the parking lot of the store, Haylee was emerging, crawling out of her funk like a moth from a cocoon. We padded through the store in our flip flops, and Nick paid for a package of blue plastic plates with a twenty from his wallet.

Haylee hugged her arms around herself, but she followed as Nick led us back to the car.

We were three blocks from the party when she pointed out the window at the first fireworks blossoming against the sky. "Stop the car!" she said.

Nick pulled over, and she scrambled out of the car and up the trunk of a palm tree to get a better look.

Nick and I stood at the base of the tree. Nick watched the fireworks sparkling above. Haylee's knees hugged the tree above us as she stretched to get closer to the explosions.

Nick stood so close to me that our arms bumped. I looked down at our hands, hanging next to each other. My fingers stretched awkwardly—how did I hold them normally? Close together? Far apart? Did I look like I wanted him to hold my hand? Did I look like I didn't? The line between available and desperate slipped through my grasp.

A particularly loud rocket burst above our heads, and I looked up to see golden streaks soaring through the air, then fading to plumes of gray smoke, leaving a ghostly relief against the dark sky.

"I don't think we're ever going to get her out of this tree," Nick said. Lights blossomed in the sky above us, and I felt the reverberation in my chest, sounding in tandem with the beating of my heart.

Nick's sleeve brushed my arm twice more before the fireworks ended, but he never took my hand.

Chapter Two

The doorknob rattled again. I stepped down off Haylee's chair and put it back at her desk before moving to the door. What was my excuse for locking it? Because I wanted to be alone?

In a dead girl's room? Kira, thy name is Morbid.

I unlocked the door and pulled it open a few inches, peeking out. Nick knelt in the hall, still wearing his collared shirt and sedate maroon tie from the burial, though it hung unevenly around his neck like he'd been tugging at it. He looked up at me, his eyes wide with surprise.

"What are you doing?" I asked. "Peeking through the keyhole?"

Nick looked at the doorknob. The lock wasn't old enough. He couldn't have peered through it if he wanted to. "Um," he said. "I'm pretty sure I was listening for a ghost."

I raised my eyebrows. "A ghost?" I asked.

Nick rubbed his forehead in embarrassment. "Yeah," he said. "That's stupid, right? I was using the bathroom and I heard a noise . . . . But I guess a person makes a lot more sense."

Was it his urine I'd been listening to? My cheeks burned. Why did I think of *that*?

"You believe in that stuff?" I asked. "Ghosts, I mean?"

Nick climbed to his feet. "No," he said. "Yes. I don't know." He gave me half a smile, digging a dimple into his left cheek. I felt my mouth turn up in mirror to his, the way people do when they're paying *way* too close attention.

I sucked my lips in, hoping he didn't notice. "Well, it's just me," I said. "Sorry to disappoint."

Nick looked surprised. "Oh," he said. "No. You don't."

I took a step back. I didn't what? Disappoint? "Well, I was just . . . I mean, I was—"

And at the same time Nick said, "I just meant—"

And then we both stood there. We'd hung out a thousand times, but always with Haylee, and apparently we'd buried our ability to interact like normal people along with her.

"Can I come in?" Nick asked finally. He looked over my shoulder, into Haylee's bedroom.

My heart double-thudded. Last night I'd picked up one of my mom's books—some pop-psychology thing on how to help your teenager through a loss. The chapter she'd earmarked was about risk-taking behaviors. It said grief loosened inhibitions, and made me more likely to take drugs, or engage in promiscuous behavior.

I wasn't exactly buying joints under the bleachers, but my heart just kept pounding, so hard I could feel it in my ears. Here we were. Nick and me. Near a bedroom. Alone. Lost friend; loose tie.

Nick cleared his throat. "Oh," he said. "I guess you probably wanted to be alone."

"No," I said. "I mean, yeah, I did. But I can be alone with you."

For the love. Why did I say *that*?

Nick's eyes widened. And for a second I thought he might flee down the stairs, running away from the crazy girl propositioning him in the bedroom full of ghosts.

He recovered quickly. "Okay," he said.

And then there was an awkward pause again, because I was

standing in the door silently, blocking his way like a freak. So I did what I should have done at the beginning of the conversation. I stepped aside and let him in. He followed, and closed the door behind him.

There wasn't a lot of room right inside Haylee's door. We both stood in the three square feet of space between her bed and her dresser. Haylee used to pull the drawers open when she didn't want her mother bursting in on her, which drove Hazel nuts. For Haylee, the annoyance was part of the charm.

Nick ran a hand through his hair, brushing it out of his eyes. Other guys smelled like hair product or body odor or—worst of all—over-done cologne, but Nick just smelled clean, with a hint of soap. I wanted to touch him, to bury my face in his chest and breathe him in. And if I hadn't been acting like such a spaz since I opened the door, I probably could have done it. Everyone else in the house seemed to be hugging.

If he'd touched me first, I might have gotten the nerve. But Nick somehow managed to stand in that space—our feet angled together, our elbows shifting about for someplace safe to be—without any part of his body touching any part of mine. He probably didn't even notice he was doing it, but I was never more aware than when Nick Harbourne was near. Like he had an invisible shield around him, he moved further into the room without so much as a brush or a bump.

So much for Mom's books. My inhibitions were as rock solid as ever. And Nick was just as oblivious.

He looked at the mess in the closet. "Were you looking for Haylee's journal?" he asked.

"Yeah," I said. Too quickly. "How did you know?"

Nick shrugged. "Aunt Hazel asked me if I knew where it was. I told her to ask you."

So that inquisition was his fault. He gave me a sideways look, and for a second, I was sure that he knew. Of course she'd told me where the journal was. I was her best friend. But the words tumbled out of my mouth. "I didn't find it. I don't know what she did with it. She didn't want me reading it either, you know?" I bit the inside of my mouth to keep even more excuses from popping out of it. I was the worst liar in the history of the world.

"Can I help you look?" he asked.

I wilted like a wet noodle. Sometimes the obliviousness worked in my favor. "Sure."

Nick surveyed the room. "Where have you looked?"

My eyes slid straight to the bottom of the closet, so I took a stab at honesty. "I was working on the closet. It's kind of a mess."

He raised an eyebrow at the piles of clothes. "No kidding," Nick said. "Have you checked under the mattress?"

I shut my eyes to keep them from rolling. Haylee would never hide her journal somewhere so unoriginal. "You check," I said.

Nick knelt down, loosening his tie further and unbuttoning his top button to expose his collar bone.

Oh, my. I dug into the clothes at the bottom of the closet, tossing them into a pile on her floor. I hadn't come to Haylee's funeral to hit on her cousin, even if that was exactly the sort of tragic romance that Haylee herself would have loved.

What I needed was a normal conversation. "Did your mom make you buy that tie for the funeral?" I asked.

"Yeah," he said. "I'm not really used to it."

"I like your T-shirts better."

Yes, Kira, I thought. *Let's talk about his wardrobe. That's not obsessive.* I grabbed Haylee's Winter Fling dress from the drawer and hung it on a hanger, where it glittered and shone. Maybe Nick would just think I'd developed a sudden obsession with clothes.

"You want to know a secret?" Nick asked. I spun around to find him unbuttoning his shirt.

I'm pretty sure my eyes nearly fell out of my head. And in a moment of pure eloquence, this one thought ran through my mind: *Whoa.*

But then I saw the rib-neck of a black T-shirt underneath

28

the buttons. He pulled the white shirt aside, revealing a red and yellow Superman symbol.

We stared at each other for a second. If Nick knew what I was thinking, he played it off without a word.

"Isn't Superman supposed to wear blue?" I asked.

"It's a Death of Superman shirt," Nick said. Looking closer, I could see that bits of the red outline were bleeding.

"I'd have thought that would show through the white shirt."

"I wore the shirt to the store. Tried on about twenty of them before I found one thick enough to cover it."

"That's ridiculous," I said.

"I know," Nick said. "I did it for Haylee."

What would Haylee have said about that? She'd have called him a dork. She *always* called Nick a dork. I was pretty sure a lot of the time he hammed it up, just for her.

"That's perfect," I said. "Who else knows?"

"Just you." He reached for his buttons.

"Don't," I said. My hand caught his before I thought about what I was doing. "Leave it." His fingers hooked through mine before I let them drop.

All the blood drained from my face. I wasn't the only one in this room who'd lost someone. If I kissed Nick right now, would he let me?

Nick sat down on the bed, no longer searching for the journal. "I wasn't really looking for a ghost up here," he said. "I mostly came up here for somewhere to be alone."

"Oh," I said. I inched toward the door. *That's* why he'd been so awkward about coming in. He was the one who'd hoped to find the room empty.

"No," he said. "You don't count."

I felt like I'd been punched in the gut. Of course I didn't count. I was like a cousin. Like his sister. Like nobody. "Okay, then."

He winced. "That's not what I meant."

I wanted to ask him what he *did* mean, but instead I just sank down beside him on the bed. Neither of us wanted to be here. We were together in that.

"Downstairs was miserable," I said.

"That," Nick said, "is the truest thing you've ever said." He leaned back on his arms, his long legs stretching to the floor. His elbows dug deep holes in the mattress, tilting me toward him. If I'd let it, gravity would have pulled me against him.

I thought about letting go, about curling up into him, and telling him about the journal. It wouldn't be the first time Nick would be my partner in crime. We'd been a team for years, passing the Haylee baton back and forth in the relay of keeping her happy.

We'd dropped it, now. If we weren't protecting her together, what were we to each other? Nothing. No wonder we didn't know how to put two sentences together anymore.

Nick played with the end of his tie, twisting it around and around. "It clashes," I said, pointing to the red of his shirt, and the maroon of his tie. "You should have found one to match."

Nick held the two colors together. "Oh," he said. "I didn't even think about it."

"Take me with you next time," I said.

Nick ducked his head, his eyes close to mine. "No," he said quietly. "Let's *never* do this again."

His hair hung from his forehead, almost brushing my own hair.

"Deal," I said. And his eyes flicked from one of mine to the other. Nick looked at me—really *looked* at me—as if he were seeing something he never had before.

And then the traitorous dust from the top of the closet finally worked its way up my nose, and I sneezed. I jerked away in time, covering my face with both hands. But when I turned back, Nick had straightened up and was re-buttoning the top of his shirt and tightening his tie.

The hairs on the back of my neck prickled. I could almost hear Haylee's voice in my ear. *Moving in on my cousin, when*

30

I'm still fresh in my grave. Are things better for you, now that I'm not around?

I chewed my lip. They weren't. I wouldn't pretend for a moment that they were.

"You want to go for a ride?" Nick asked. "Get out of here for a while?"

I drew a deep breath. I wanted to. Of course I wanted to. I'd been going out of my way to sit by him and walk by him and smile at him for years. Maybe he was thinking the same thing I was—that this was his big chance to . . . what? Make a move? Take advantage?

Would I mind?

Yes, I would.

Nothing good was going to come out of Haylee's death. I wouldn't let it.

"I better not," I said. "My mom's downstairs." That was only half of an excuse. I tried to think of a follow up, but my mind went blank.

"I'd steal the plates," Nick said, "but I'm not sure anyone would notice, today."

I smiled. "Raincheck," I said. "Okay?"

Nick smiled back, and if I'd been feeling more hopeful, I might have said it was a mirror of mine. "Okay," he said.

Nick held out his hand. "Come downstairs with me? I don't think I can face it alone."

I reached up and took his hand, and he pulled me up off the bed, and then dropped it again, like the gesture meant nothing. Like I was his cousin, same as Haylee. Only a more distant one. Many times removed.

So far removed as to be easily forgotten.

He turned toward the door, and I allowed myself one glance back up at the crawlspace.

I could insist that I didn't want to go downstairs. I could try to get rid of Nick. But I'd still have the same problem—I had no way to get the journal out of the house.

31

I'd have to come back. And next time, I'd bring a purse.

I stumbled out of the room behind Nick. But as I did, I could swear I felt the swish of cold air behind my ear, like Haylee had swept out of her room with us.

I glanced over my shoulder, half convinced I'd see Haylee's ghost, but all I saw behind me was the empty hall. Haylee wasn't free. She was locked in a box, smothered under rocks and the dirt.

But I could feel her, still behind me no matter which way I turned. *Good thing you hid that journal,* she said. *You had to cover your tracks.*

Didn't you?

Haylee had always known which words would cut deepest, though that power was stronger in memory than it had been in real life. She was so much meaner in my head.

And now the Haylee in my head was the only one I had left.

Ten Days Before

I sat on Haylee's floor. "Three weeks until Christmas break," I said.

Haylee lay on her bed with her copy of *Tess of the D'Urbervilles* splayed open across her face. Her hair cascaded out from underneath it in waves of ringlet curls, which had defied gravity by maintaining their bounce through the entire school day. Mine would have been limp inside of an hour.

"Don't remind me," Haylee said. "Only eight days until that stupid dance. I don't even have a dress yet. Why did I agree to go again?"

I threw a ruffled throw pillow at her head. "Calm down. You're crazy about him."

Haylee batted the pillow away without disturbing her hair. "I suppose if Nick had asked you, you'd be totally relaxed."

She was right. I'd be a wreck. "Who *did* Nick ask?"

Haylee peeked out from under the book. "Why?" she asked. "Jealous?"

"No," I said. "But yes."

Haylee's satisfied smile peeked out from under the book's spine. "Relax. He didn't ask anybody."

I rolled my eyes. "I wouldn't say that's good news."

"Please," Haylee said. "He'll wake up to your gorgeousness

eventually. The guy isn't blind."

It had been enough years. Maybe he was.

"This wasn't my point," I said. "My mom will be home the whole break. It'll be just me and her and our tiny house."

The book across Haylee's face teetered as she spoke. "You're not going anywhere?"

"I'll be going insane."

Haylee lifted the corner of the book and glanced at me. "It won't be that bad."

I threw my arms out to the sides, clocking one of my hands on Haylee's dresser. "Me and Mom, stuck in the house together for a whole break. I'll be smothered by the silence." How two people could be related to each other and have so little to say was beyond me. I could always think of lots of things to say to Haylee. "I'm going to come over here every day. Or better yet, you should let me sleep over. Every night."

"Sorry," Haylee said, waving her book at me. "But I'm not going to survive until Christmas break. This paper is going to kill me."

"Please," I said. "At least you read it."

Haylee rolled her eyes at me. "One of us had to."

I hadn't finished a book for English class in over two years. "What's the point? You spoil them all."

"It is *not* my fault. You are the only person in the history of the world who made it to fourteen years old without knowing that Romeo and Juliet die."

"Seriously," I said. "What kind of a love story is that?"

"It's a tragedy," Haylee said. "That's the best kind." Haylee let her copy of *Tess* fall to the floor, on top of her flannel pajama pants covered in rubber duckies.

I picked it up and leafed through it. It wasn't like I was *trying* to cheat off of Haylee. I'd read the first chapter, and been bored to tears. But Haylee devoured every book we were assigned in two days.

Except the *Grapes of Wrath*. That one took her three.

"I thought this was a tragedy, too," I said, scanning the back cover. "It says Tess gets jilted. That's totally your thing."

"It is!" Haylee said. "That's the problem. I can't write about Tess. I *am* Tess."

I read the blurb further. "Were you raped?" I asked. "And are you pregnant?"

Haylee balled up her pillow in her hands. "I'm doomed," Haylee said quietly. "Just like Tess."

"Right. So if you're so similar, can't you just do whatever she did to get out of it?"

"She kills the guy, and even that doesn't help her escape from what he did to her."

I waved the book at her. "She's a *murderer*? That's how it ends?"

"Don't get pissy. You weren't going to read it."

I should have known. Books we read for English class never ended well. "Don't follow *that* example."

Haylee snatched the book from my hands. "You just don't *understand*," she said. "She kills Alec because it's her only means of destroying the part of herself that she hates."

"Yes," I said. I let the sarcasm weigh in my voice. "You clearly had a lot in common."

Haylee bit her lip, staring at the book.

Somewhere, we'd crossed over the line from joking to serious, but I wasn't sure where it had been. "Sorry," I said.

"No, you're right," she said, tearing the corner of the cover with her nail. "Obviously Tess is nothing like me."

"And that's a good thing," I said. "Right?"

"Sure," Haylee said.

But I could tell that she didn't believe it.

Chapter Three

Monday morning I cruised by Bradley Johansen's locker before class, but he wasn't there. We had English together—with Haylee as well—but that wasn't until the end of the day.

I paced the hallway back and forth until the first bell, but Bradley didn't appear. I waited so long that I had to run to geometry, and slid into my seat just as the second bell rung. Usually Mr. Craig would have given me the evil eye for that, but today he smiled like he was glad to see me.

We had a big test scheduled for Wednesday, the last day before Christmas break. But I could tell from all the whispering and fidgeting that I wasn't the only one who couldn't bring myself to care. My eyes kept drifting toward the empty desk next to me. When Mr. Craig was scanning the room for the roll, I saw his eyes pause on the desk, too, but he didn't mark Haylee absent.

"Counselors are still available for anyone who needs to talk," Mr. Craig said. "They'll be here until the end of the week." He'd said the same thing last week, and neither time did he mention what we might need to talk about.

Once Mr. Craig finished his public service announcement, he moved straight to math. "We're going to pair up for the review problems," he said. "Talk through the problems together, and then check with the answers in the back of the book. If you got a different answer, try to figure it out together first before you ask for help."

My classmates all started turning around in their seats, finding partners. Mr. Craig divided us up a lot, so everyone pretty much had a steady partner. I forced myself not to look at the space where Haylee should be. Every other empty desk in the room was taken, or turned around, or shoved out of the way.

But no one moved Haylee's. It just sat there, facing forward. I wondered if her ghost sat in its seat. If I touched it, would it be cold?

"Kira," Mr. Craig said. "Why don't you work with Spencer?" He said it like it was a casual thing, but he hadn't assigned a partner to anyone else.

I stared down at my hands. Spencer, of all people. If I didn't make eye contact, would he find someone else? Maybe there was an odd number of people in the class. Maybe Mr. Craig would let me work by myself.

But no. Spencer trundled across the room and threw his backpack down on Haylee's desk. It wasn't that Spencer was stupid—he could actually be really smart if he stopped practicing his stand-up routine long enough to pay attention. Unfortunately for him, he wasn't that funny.

It could have been worse. I could have been paired up with Stephanie. She was sure to spend the entire period flirting with anything male in a three-desk radius.

Spencer kicked back in Haylee's seat, with his feet propped up on the edge of my chair. "All right," he said, flipping open his own book. "Let the learning begin."

I looked at Spencer's book. He'd opened to a chapter we'd covered in October. "Do you even know where we are?"

"Sure," he said, rifling through some pages. "Um, proofs?"

"There are proofs in every chapter."

"So I'm not wrong."

"Chapter nine," I said, opening to the chapter review. My

grip tightened on my pencil. I was used to helping Haylee, but Spencer was different. I'd rather fail the test than do his homework for him. "Let's just do the problems and compare answers, okay?"

"Sure thing, boss." Spencer bent over, rummaging through his backpack.

I was halfway through the first problem when he tapped me on the arm. "Uh, Kira? Do you have a piece of paper I could borrow?"

I tore an extra sheet out of my notebook and thrust it at him. Fringes from the spiral binding fluttered to the floor.

"Thanks," he said, taking it from me. "Do you have a pencil?"

I pulled one out of my backpack, holding it out to him without looking at him. "Anything else?"

"Nah, thanks."

I nodded, and went back to my problem. It took Spencer about three seconds to start talking again.

"So, do you know how she did it?"

The problems swam before my eyes. I was not having that conversation in the middle of math. "No."

"Aw, come on. You were her best friend. You must know something."

I couldn't tell if he was curious, or just trying to annoy me. Gripping my pencil, I tried to keep my tone even. "Nope. Nobody tells me anything."

Spencer paused, and I thought for a futile second that he might just drop it.

"Don't you think it's strange that nobody knows?"

I ground my pencil in a tight circle around the binder hole on my paper. "No," I said. "They're afraid if they tell us how she did it, we'll all try it." My mom said suicide was contagious, as if whatever was wrong with Haylee could pass from person to person like the chicken pox.

Spencer leaned toward me and whispered. "Some of us think maybe she didn't really do it. Maybe someone else killed her and the suicide thing is a cover up."

"You watch too much CSI," I said.

"No, really. I mean, didn't she go out with Bradley right before she died? Maybe he did it. I heard the principal called him into his office to talk about—"

I'd ground the lead of my pencil nearly down to a stump. I should have realized everyone at school would be wondering about Haylee and Bradley. They'd been seen in public together at the dance. No wonder Bradley was hiding. "Do the proof," I said.

Spencer just could not get the hint. "Or maybe her parents did it. I mean, why would Haylee—"

"Shut up," I said. "Her parents had *nothing* to do with it. This was Haylee's choice, okay?" I gripped my pencil even harder, so hard I was afraid it might splinter in my hand. Then at least I could go to the nurse.

Did I really feel that way? Did I really blame Haylee for what she'd done? I wasn't sure. But I was certain I didn't want to hash those feelings out with *Spencer*.

My hands went cold. The only person I wanted to talk about it with was Haylee.

Spencer went on like I hadn't even spoken. "Maybe—"

Lynette Handley reached from behind Spencer and whacked him on the back of the head.

Spencer rubbed the back of his hair. "Hey! What's that for?"

Lynette glared at him. "Spencer, why are you such a dickwad?"

At least I wasn't the only one he was pissing off.

He looked at her all wide-eyed. "What'd I do?"

"You're freaking clueless. Leave her alone."

I hunched my shoulders over my paper, trying to focus on the diagram in front of me. The numbers slipped in and out of my mind like they were coated in Vaseline. I dug my nails into the paint on my pencil.

Christmas break couldn't come fast enough.

As I finished the proof, I could feel Spencer looking at my paper over my shoulder. He scrawled something down on his own paper. I was pretty sure my answer was wrong, so copying wasn't going to help him. I heard the lead on his pencil—my pencil—snap, and he leaned over to me again. "Got a sharpener?"

"No."

Spencer got up, jammed my pencil into the wall-sharpener, and wound the handle around, grinding away. I'd be lucky if I got it back with more than a stub left.

I lifted my head to find Mr. Craig sitting at his desk, studying me. When I met his eyes, he smiled. I thought about smiling back, so he'd think I was okay and leave me alone, but the corners of my mouth felt like they were tacked down.

Spencer plunked himself back down in Haylee's seat, and started to open his mouth. If he said one more thing to me, I was going to put my pencil right through his eye. Spencer was always annoying, but he'd never provoked me to violence before, which meant I was being more pissy than normal. I wondered if "bitch" was one of the stages of grief.

I stood up out of my seat before Spencer could get more than a syllable out of his mouth, and marched over to Mr. Craig's desk. "Can I go to the bathroom?" I asked.

Mr. Craig looked up at me. "How are you doing?"

"Fine." Fine was my new best friend. The magical F word that really meant *I don't want to talk about it*, but didn't sound as rude.

"Have you thought about seeing the counselor?"

"I just want to go to the bathroom."

Mr. Craig nodded. "Take the pass."

I walked out the door without saying anything to Spencer, grabbing the hall pass on my way—a toilet seat, complete with lid. I think Mr. Craig did that so nobody would steal it. It's pretty hard to lose something that tacky.

I kept my eyes glued to the floor, following the ugly rows of green and orange tiles, lining my feet up so that I stepped directly in the center of each square. I was so intent on it that I didn't register that someone was calling my name until I'd already passed him.

"Kira? Hello?"

I whirled around.

Nick stood in the middle of the hall, waving. "Hey," he said. "How's it going?" His eyes flicked to the toilet seat.

"Hall pass," I said. But I twisted it around behind my back, so he wouldn't stare.

"Mr. Craig?"

So it was infamous. "Yeah," I said. "Geometry. What are you doing?"

Nick waved a paper at me. "Taking the roll to the office." Nick was wearing a T-shirt with a picture of a digital clock on it. As I watched, the design shifted, ticking off the seconds. I blinked. What looked like a logo was actually a glowing digital clock embedded in the cotton.

Then I realized I was totally staring at Nick's pecs. That's why I couldn't wear shirts like that. I'd be giving guys license to look at my chest.

Nick looked down at his shirt and smiled. "Awesome, huh?"

Yes, I thought, *that's totally the reason I'm staring.* "How does it work?"

Nick stepped close to me. He pulled a battery pack out of his pocket. A plastic cord ran up into the hem.

I tugged on the pack, and the outline of the cord tensed under his shirt.

He smiled as my hand brushed his, and I got so lost in his eyes that I nearly fell over.

I looked up at the ceiling, keeping my feet planted on the floor. "How do you wash it?" I asked.

Great, Kira. Let's talk about laundry. That didn't make me the most boring girl in history.

"It's detachable," Nick said. "Hey, after you left the reception, my mom and I went through some more of Haylee's room

41

looking for the journal."

Oh, no. Oh no, no, no. I tried to smile casually, but I was pretty sure it came out as a menacing grimace. "Did you find it?"

He shook his head. "Not yet. We were just trying to do Aunt Hazel a favor, so she wouldn't have to do it. But I felt pretty creepy going through Haylee's stuff."

If Haylee hadn't already died literally, she would have died figuratively from having a guy dig around in her room, cousin or no. "Maybe I could help you look sometime," I said.

Nick shook his head. "Hazel said she wanted to do it, though I don't really see why. It's depressing in there."

Ugh. There went my chance. If I couldn't get in there to help, I at least needed to distract them. "Maybe Haylee threw the journal out," I said. My cheeks burned, which was what I was pretty sure my soul was going to do as a punishment for this lie. "You know, since she planned this, I guess."

"Maybe," Nick said. And as he stared at his Vans, I knew he was thinking about those last hours of Haylee's life, about what she must have been thinking. He had to be asking the same question I was.

If she thought about this ahead of time, why didn't she talk to me?

"I'm sorry," I said.

"Don't be," Nick said. His hand hesitated in the air, then dropped to his side.

The number of ways this boy could *not* touch me was truly astounding.

We looked at each other for a moment, and finally Nick said, "Are you okay?"

The hall was so silent, you could have heard his clock tick, if it hadn't been digital. Did he mean right now, or in general? Either way, that question had both a million answers, and none. I went with the F word. "Fine, I guess."

He nodded, even though I was pretty sure he knew that I wasn't. "We could talk sometime, if you want."

If only I could stop spouting lies long enough to carry on a normal conversation. "Maybe," I said.

Nick cringed a little. "I mean, you don't have to if you don't want to."

"No, I do," I said, cutting him off. "I didn't mean to say that I didn't. I just—"

"I'll call you later, then, okay?"

He'd call me later. *Nick Harbourne* would call me later. "Okay," I said.

Nick gave me a half-wave, then turned and walked down the hall.

Smooth, Kira. A truly brilliant performance. No doubt Nick would be dreaming about me, now.

In his weirdest nightmares.

I stomped the rest of the way to the bathroom. Before, running in to Nick was easy enough. I'd never needed an excuse to see him—I could just tag along whenever his family got together with Haylee's. I was practically another cousin. Maybe we weren't friends exactly, but he didn't seem to be repulsed by spending time with me. Things were normal. I knew how to handle normal.

I shoved open the bathroom doors. Now talking to Nick felt like stepping into one of Haylee's plays, only I didn't know my blocking or my lines.

I splashed cold water on my face, and gripped the edge of the sink. I needed to process this, to parse every detail of what he said. Later, when I told the story to—

Oh.

Oh, no. No, no, no.

How could I forget even for a moment? I would never, never tell this story.

There was no one to tell.

One Week After

The hardness of the bench seats alone should have been enough to make me cry at Haylee's funeral, but my traitorous eyes stayed dry. As the minister droned on, my mother sniffled and tugged tissues from the mini-pack in her purse. Two rows ahead of me, I could see the girl who sat two tables away from us at lunch pawing at her eyes with her sleeve. In the front row, I could see Hazel crying into Aaron's shoulder. He turned once, to look at something behind me. His eyes were rimmed with red.

I tried not to blink through the service. If my eyes stayed open long enough, surely they'd start to water. But my mouth was parched. I was shriveling up like a raisin. My body might be seventy percent water, but not one drop of it collected in my eyes.

I wished I was Haylee. She cried at everything—movies, failed tests, imagined insults. Sometimes at nothing.

She didn't have to sit here, not knowing what to do next. She didn't have to face the next days—weeks, months, *years*—without her.

The funeral was easiest for the corpse.

Chapter Four

My last-period English class was the only other class I shared with Haylee, and I walked toward it as slowly as I could. The last thing I wanted to look at was another empty desk.

When I arrived, I found a seating chart on the white board. The chart showed no empty seats. One of the desks in the room had been removed. Ms. Roxburg must not have wanted to look at Haylee's desk any more than I did. But this was worse than the empty desk: it had only been a week, and now Haylee's space would be not just empty, but erased.

The room was already full, so it wasn't hard to find my seat, on the opposite side of the classroom from where I used to sit. Bradley Johansen was supposed to sit directly in front of me, but his desk was empty.

When Ms. Roxburg walked to the front of the room to start class, Bradley's seat was still empty. He had to be avoiding me.

No, that was the kind of self-centered thinking Haylee always got trapped in. Bradley barely knew I existed—he wouldn't skip school just to avoid me. He might be sick.

Or maybe he'd done something cruel to Haylee, and he felt too guilty to come to school. Spencer said the principal had talked to him. Had he been suspended?

Unless he'd been expelled, or fled the country, he had to come back to school eventually. But what if he skipped the next two days, and didn't come back until after the break? I couldn't wait two and a half weeks to confront him.

I spent class staring at the back of Bradley's chair, as if I could will him into it. Before I knew it, the last bell was ringing. Ms. Roxburg must have noticed that I was dazed through her class, but she'd let it slide. I wondered how long my free pass to bad classroom behavior would last.

Hopefully a while, since I had no intention of writing that essay about Tess.

After school, I walked over to Haylee's house. This time I had my backpack, so I'd have someplace to put the journal. If it was true that Hazel was actively searching for it, I couldn't afford to leave it in the crawl space forever.

On a normal day I would have walked right in, even though Hazel hated it when I did that. Haylee didn't live here anymore, so I rang the doorbell. The Ricks had one of those tune doorbells—the kind you can set to play one of eight different songs. This time of year, Hazel set it to "Jingle Bells."

For a long minute I thought no one would answer the door, but then the curtains stirred in the front window and I saw Hazel peek out at me. She opened the door looking even worse than she had at the funeral. Before, the bright makeup made her features look painted on, but today she hadn't bothered to put any on, and her hair pulled back from her face in a tight bun, making her look pinched and faded.

"Hi, Kira," she said. She didn't step aside to let me in, like she would have if Haylee were home.

"Hey," I said. "Um, I'm here because I think I left something in Haylee's room a while ago. My math book. Can I go up to her room to check?"

"Oh," Hazel said. "I've already packed up her books and given them to the school. If yours was with them, they probably have it."

Hazel sure got right on that. That was like her, though. She couldn't stand leaving things undone.

"Do you think I can go up and look anyway?" I said. "Maybe you missed it. It wasn't with the others."

Hazel sighed. "I'm sorry," she said, already beginning to close the door. "Now really isn't a good time."

I bounced on the balls of my feet, like I was eight years old, asking for Haylee to come out to play. "I'll be quiet. I won't bother you at all."

Hazel's voice dropped. "Haylee's father stayed home from work," she said. "And he's really not up for visitors."

I wasn't a visitor. He was my coach; I was practically his second daughter. I'd been calling him by his first name for years. But that didn't stop Hazel from closing the door in my face.

Three Weeks Before

When cross-country ended, Haylee and I started walking home together again. On a Tuesday, Ms. Roxburg stopped me to discuss an in-class essay I'd faked my way through based on Haylee's description of the first few chapters of *Tess*. Haylee went ahead to my locker, but came back to meet me at the classroom door with a scowl on her face.

"What's up?" I asked.

Haylee gave me a look to end all looks. "You have to see this," she said. "I have no words."

She marched me down the hallway and around the corner. There, square on my locker, were Bradley Johansen and Fiona Gil, her legs wrapped around his waist, and his hands on either side of her, pinning her to the locker door. Their heads tilted to opposite sides, and their lips locked together like Lincoln Logs. Fiona's skirt had slid all the way up to the top of her thighs, and only Bradley's torso blocked our view of the underwear I sincerely hoped she was wearing.

"Ew," I said.

Haylee sighed.

I walked up three lockers away and cleared my throat, but I don't think they could hear me over the sound of the sucking of their own faces.

I mentally counted through the books in my locker. There wasn't anything in there I *had* to have. But when I looked back at Haylee, I found her shrinking against the opposite bank of lockers.

No one did that to my best friend.

I moved even closer and knocked on Karen Tran's locker, right next to mine.

Fiona's eyes popped open, and she had to turn her face ninety degrees to separate herself from Bradley.

"Move," I said.

Fiona's legs dropped to the ground, and Bradley took a step back. He glanced at me, only then seeming to notice my presence. "Sorry, Kira," he said. He pulled Fiona away from my locker by her tank-top strap, revealing a full cup of her bra as he led her toward the door to the parking lot.

I looked at my locker. I was sure this wasn't the first time someone had copped a feel against it, but I still didn't want to touch it.

Haylee crossed the hallway and slammed her back against Karen's locker, propping herself at a forty-five degree angle to the floor with her feet.

"Can you believe that?" she asked.

"No," I said. I didn't see how anyone could do anything so intimate in the halls of the school. By the end of the day, they always smelled like six flavors of BO. Not exactly a turn on.

But when I looked at Haylee, she was staring dreamily off into space. She turned to me, and gave me a half-smile. "He could kiss me like that anytime."

Chapter Five

The first night of winter break, I could smell Mom making hot chocolate—the good kind with real chocolate that she melted on the stove. She was probably hoping the aroma would beckon to me. I wanted to fight it, but the pull of steamy chocolate was too strong. I let my feet carry me into the kitchen.

Mom was still in her work clothes—black slacks and an off-white collared blouse. She'd wound her orange chiffon scarf around the back of one of the kitchen chairs. She smiled at me as I stood in the doorway, and pointed to bottles of flavoring on the counter.

"Mocha or mint?" she asked. "Or something else?"

I scrutinized the bottles. "Hazelnut?"

"Hazelnut it is."

Mom stirred the chocolate, watching it carefully. She'd put the flavoring in at the very end, since it didn't need to cook.

"Do you want to go see a movie tomorrow?" she asked without looking up at me.

"I don't know," I said. Mom liked to go to movies about women who got cancer or whose mothers had nervous breakdowns. I couldn't do it. Even a mindless disaster movie would feature too much death.

"I just thought," Mom said, still stirring, "that it might get your mind off things."

If people wanted to get my mind off things, they'd stop reminding me to get my mind off them. Besides, I wasn't entirely sure I *should*. If your best friend died, that seemed like the sort of thing that ought to stay on your mind for a while.

"We could even go tonight, if you want," Mom said. She pulled out two mugs and poured in the chocolate, followed by flavoring. She had to shake the hazelnut bottle to squeeze out the last drops. "It's not a school night."

I shrugged. "I think I'm going to practice."

"At night?" Mom asked, blowing on the top of her drink. "The neighbors don't like that."

"They went to their cabin for Christmas," I said.

She took a sip, and nodded. "So they did."

"Thanks for the chocolate," I said, and I turned to take it up to my room.

"Kira?" Mom said.

I winced. Here it was. The lecture about how I wasn't handling my feelings appropriately. The plea for me to tell her what I was thinking. The suggestion that I ought to talk to a therapist, as if that ever helped Haylee.

But when I pivoted back, Mom was staring down into her chocolate. "Yes?" I asked.

"I'm here if you need to talk," she said.

Mom talked to kids at the middle school all day long about their problems. That was her job as the school psychologist. She had to attend meeting after meeting about behavior modification plans, resources, and support. It wasn't really her fault that talking to teenagers put her into therapy mode. Fixing kids was her job. When I was in middle school, the teachers used to tell me how lucky I was to have a mother who really understood.

But they were wrong. The only person who understood me was Haylee.

"Thanks, Mom," I said. And I turned and walked up the

stairs. A few drops of chocolate sloshed over the edge of the mug, stinging my thumb.

Up in my room, I let the hot chocolate cool on my night-stand, and picked up my cell phone. It hadn't rung much over the last week. Even Nick hadn't called.

At this point, there was only one other person I wanted to talk to.

Bradley Johansen.

I had Bradley's number from an English project we all did in September. Haylee talked my ear off all day about him, but when we all worked together on the project, she didn't say word one. If she kept that up on their date, it was no wonder she didn't want to talk to me about it.

I dialed, and the phone rang in my ear: once, twice, three times. I'd called before, so I probably looked like a stalker. But it wasn't until this time that I realized he probably didn't have my number in his phone anymore. If I didn't recognize the number that was calling, I wouldn't pick up, either.

That meant I ought to leave a message. "This is Kira," I said to his voicemail. "I want to talk to you about . . . things."

Things? *Things?* Brilliant. I paused, trying to think of what to say next, but I'd already trailed a silence behind my genius statement, so I hung up.

I hoped Bradley wasn't one of those people who never checked their messages.

My cocoa was cool enough to drink, so I downed it and threw on some warm-ups and sneakers, grabbed my glove, and headed downstairs and out the back door.

The moon and stars were out, but as I flipped on the back light they seemed to dim. We lived in a townhouse, so our backyard was really more of a patio. There wasn't much room, but if I stood on one side and tossed a softball against the far fence, I had just enough space for pitching practice. I'd been playing softball since I was eight for the local community league. Try-outs for the high school teams were in January—we all had to do them again, even if we were on last year's team. I'd been a relief pitcher last season, which was better than not pitching at all. If I made starting pitcher this year, I'd be in good shape for the Varsity team as a junior.

Mom and I had propped a board against the fence and outlined a square on it with blue electrical tape, about the right size and height for a strike zone. I wished I could go over to practice with Aaron, since practicing with a person was so much better than practicing with a fence.

My stomach dropped. Maybe he'd found the journal. If he had, we'd never practice together again.

I dragged my bucket of balls over and looked at the strike square. I set, then swung my arm around and stepped forward, releasing the ball, feeling the familiar pop of my hip. The ball hit the fence about two feet to the left of the square.

I kicked myself for not practicing more. I needed to warm up, sure, but I'd never get to start if I threw like that.

Ball after ball thwacked against the fence. Too high. Too low. Inside. Outside. I stopped to take a deep breath, trying to figure out what I was doing wrong. Aaron said it was no use continuing to throw bad pitches, because I'd only teach myself to do it wrong.

I stood with my right shoulder to the fence and set again. Nothing else matters, I told myself. Just me and the ball.

The next one hit the left edge of the square with a satisfying smack. Not perfect, but better.

I emptied the bucket, then picked up all the balls and emptied it again. It felt good to be moving. After fifty pitches or so I got into my groove, and ball after ball hit the square. I started focusing on putting the ball where I wanted it: high left, low right, dead center, high center. I smiled to myself. At last, something I could control. I emptied the bucket one more time and stood there, looking at the balls that had rolled all over the concrete.

If I stood very still, the night seemed like any other. I could finish practice, shower, and run over to Haylee's house for an hour or two. It wasn't even a school night. I could sleep over if I wanted. We could watch movies until dawn and then sleep until noon.

But I couldn't do that ever again.

I sat down on the concrete, staring at my pitching square. The ground leached heat out of my legs through my warm-ups. I stared up at the moon, refusing to blink. If I just got my eyes started, like priming a pump, then surely I could cry. But my eyes just felt stiff, like I'd spent hours in a car with the windows down.

A chill brushed over me, and I could hear Haylee's voice in my head, clear as anything.

I would have cried, if you were the one who was dead.

And if that thought didn't make me cry, I didn't know what would.

I was halfway up the stairs when I heard my phone ringing in my room. I jogged up the remaining steps and threw my door open, grabbing my phone just in time to see Bradley's name.

"Hello?" I said.

"Hey, Kira," Bradley said.

But my brain didn't recalibrate fast enough, so I was all, "Oh, hi, Bradley! This is, um, Kira." And not only did I sound like I couldn't remember my name, but he had just said it himself.

But Bradley didn't seem to notice. He just said, "I got your message. What's up?"

If he'd hurt Haylee, shouldn't he sound guilty? I'd been sure he was avoiding me, and now here he was, calling me like we were friends. "Um," I said. "I called you a couple times."

"Sorry," he said. "If I'd realized it was you, I would have answered. I'd been expecting to hear from you. About Haylee."

Really? "You weren't at the funeral."

"Yeah, sorry about that. My mom wouldn't let me go. She wants me to lie low, since I was the last person to really spend time with Haylee. She says it looks bad. But I think that's crap,

54

you know? A girl I went out with is dead. I should at least have shown up to her funeral."

Now I really didn't know what to say. He sounded like a guy Haylee had put in a bad situation, not a guy who was responsible for her death.

"Can you hold on a minute?" Bradley asked.

"Sure," I said. I listened to the silence on the other end of the phone, taking a moment to breathe. Right when I was thinking that maybe if I hung up on him he wouldn't call back, and maybe he'd forget about it by January when we went back to school, he picked up the phone again.

"Sorry. My mom just got home. I walked upstairs so she wouldn't hear."

"Oh, okay," I said.

"Are you all right?" he asked.

There was a big long pause, because I didn't know how to answer that question. Should I give him the F word, or should I tell him the truth? And what was the truth, anyway? How *was* I? That's when I realized I must be going absolutely crazy, because I couldn't answer the simplest of questions.

I dropped the F-bomb: "I'm fine." But right at that moment he decided to say something else so I ended up talking over him. We both laughed, though my laugh sounded fake, and I wondered if he noticed.

"Sorry," I said. "I'm a little out of it."

"I get that."

"So why weren't you at school?"

Bradley sighed. "My mom is freaking out. The cops came by my house the night after it happened."

So I wasn't the only one who thought he was suspicious. "Are you serious?" I asked.

"Yeah. I told them everything I could. They wanted to know if anything happened, you know? If I knew why she did it."

I sucked in my breath. "What did you tell them?"

"I didn't know what to say. I keep going over the night in my

55

head, trying to figure it out. Did I do something or say something? But I don't know what could have set her off."

My grip loosened on the phone. "I know how that is," I said. "Haylee didn't always need a reason to get upset." I bit my lip. I didn't like talking about Haylee in the past tense, and I didn't like talking behind her back, even if she couldn't possibly find out.

Bradley just breezed on. "So my mom wanted me to stay home until after the break. She thinks if I do that, everything will blow over."

My grip tightened on the phone again. "She thinks people will forget Haylee. She *wants* them to."

Bradley sighed. "I know. It's crap, like I said. Not that I want people to think I did something to her, but it seems pretty self-serving to want people to forget her just so they don't talk behind my back."

The silence stretched on and on, but I didn't know how to break it. Bradley didn't know what happened to her any better than I did. He was just another dead end.

I'd started working on ways to get out of the conversation gracefully when Bradley said, "Do you want to hang out tomorrow?"

I swallowed. I couldn't hold a five minute phone conversation. How would I handle talking to him in person?

"Cause I've had my license over six months," he said. "I can pick you up."

I'd forgotten that Bradley was older than the rest of us. His parents sent him to kindergarten a year late so he'd be old for his grade and have a better chance at sports. And I guess it worked, because Bradley made varsity last year, while I was on JV with the rest of the freshmen.

"Kira?" he asked. "Are you still there?"

"Yeah," I said. And to save us from another big long pause, I said, "Sure. Let's get together."

"You must miss Haylee a lot."

I hesitated, and then said, "Yeah, I do."

"Yeah," he said. "This sucks."

For some reason, that was the first response to Haylee's death that I appreciated. He wasn't trying to tell me he understood, or make me feel better. He just made the obvious statement. Haylee's death sucked. Like a wet vac. Like a whirlpool. Like a freaking class five tornado.

"So, I'll pick you up at noon, okay?"

I said okay, and we both hung up. I sat on the floor of my room, with my phone still to my ear. I half expected Bradley to call back and tell me he was just kidding. Why would he want to hang out with me?

But even if Bradley hadn't caused Haylee's death, he might know things he didn't even know that he knew. He wasn't close to Haylee. He didn't know how to read her.

There was still hope to find out what happened through him. I just needed to get him to tell me everything that happened, detail by detail.

And first, I had to figure out how to pitch this to my mother.

Two Weeks Before

When I walked into Haylee's room, she was sitting on the edge of her bed, holding her phone to her ear. She was wearing a pink skirt covered in clear sequins that she'd sewn on one by one over the summer. When she saw me she bounced a little on the bed and flapped her free hand in front of her face.

Bradley, she mouthed at me.

I must have looked doubtful, because she followed it with *Really!*

I had reason to doubt. He barely knew she existed, and it had been, what? Not even a week since we'd seen him suctioned simultaneously to my locker and Fiona Gil's face?

"That sounds great," she said into the phone. "I'd love to go."

Where? I mouthed at her. I flopped down on the bed next to Haylee, leaning against her, trying to hear the other side of the conversation.

Haylee grinned so wide I thought her face might cramp up. "Okay. Right. I'll see you Monday. Okay. Bye." Haylee punched the off button on the phone and squealed.

"What's going on?"

"Bradley asked me to the Winter Fling!" Haylee buried her face in a pillow and squealed again, then rolled over to judge my reaction.

I let the information soak in. The real shocker wasn't so much that he'd asked her, but that he'd stopped sucking face with Fiona Gil long enough to make a phone call. "Did he break up with Fiona? I didn't hear about it."

Haylee's smile faded a little. "I don't know," she said. She fiddled with a comforter corner. "He must have, right? Maybe over Thanksgiving break."

"Maybe," I said. It wouldn't be the first time they split.

Haylee bit her lip. "He must have, right? He can't really two-time her at the school dance without her knowing."

That was the truth.

Haylee leaned slowly back on her pillow. "You're right. It was probably a joke or something."

Ugh. I deserved to be slapped for taking all the punch out of Haylee's moment. What kind of a best friend was I? I forced a smile on my face. "Don't be stupid," I said. "He asked you, didn't he? Where's the joke in that?"

Haylee shrugged. "He sounded like he meant it."

"Of course he did." I tried to silence my doubts, but they crept in anyway. This was the second biggest dance of the year, next to Prom, and Prom was only for juniors and seniors.

"But why would he ask me? He's never noticed me before."

"Well," I said, throwing as much enthusiasm into my voice as I could, "maybe he has, and you just didn't know it." I fiddled with the edge of Haylee's comforter. Bradley wasn't exactly the love-from-afar type. He was focused—the kind of guy who reached for what he wanted and got it every time. He was our middle school valedictorian. He starred in every baseball team he played on, and still had time to be on student council.

Haylee spoke as if she were measuring her words with her tongue. "Bradley Johansen asked me to Winter Fling."

But her happiness dissolved like a sandcastle as the tide came in. She flopped onto her back, grabbing her black beret from her bedpost and pulling it low over her forehead. "Kira! I can't go with him. What would I say? No, what would I wear?"

"I'll help you," I said. "We'll find you a dress. Think your parents will pay for one?"

"Yeah," Haylee said. "Probably. Mom always says I should go to more dances."

Or, you know. Any. "See? No problem."

"But what will I say to him all night? I don't know how to talk to guys."

"You'll figure it out. Just be yourself." I cringed. That was one of those pieces of advice Mom gave that didn't actually mean anything.

"You'll go shopping with me, right? And help me figure out what I'm going to say?"

"Yeah, of course."

"And this can't kill me."

Fiona might, if she came to the dance freshly dumped. She could easily snare a new date between now and then. I wouldn't be there; Haylee would have to face the cat fight alone.

She looked at me hopefully, still waiting for my response. And more than anything, I didn't want to be responsible for a puddle of Haylee, so I gave her the answer she wanted. "Kill you?" I asked. "Are you kidding me? You're going to have a blast."

"Right," Haylee said. "I'll have the time of my life."

But no matter how hard I tried, I just couldn't picture it.

Chapter Six

The next day when I came down for breakfast at 8:30, Mom looked up at me in surprise.

"I thought you'd sleep in today," she said.

"I did," I said.

She glanced at the clock. "A little."

I shrugged. "I can go back to bed if you want."

"No," Mom said. "Have you thought about that movie?"

I grabbed a packaged muffin from the cupboard and toyed with the wrapper. I'd practiced the wording before I came downstairs, making sure to leave gender out of it. I wasn't allowed to date until I turned sixteen, and I wouldn't be sixteen until June. Granted, hanging out with Bradley wasn't a date, but I didn't think Mom was going to see it that way. "Actually," I said, "a friend wants to hang out today."

Mom's face lit up, like I knew it would. She'd been dying for me to have friends who weren't Haylee, even before.

Now for the bombshell. "He said he'd come by at noon." I buried my head in the refrigerator and pulled out the butter.

"He?" Mom raised her eyebrows. "Do I know him?"

"I don't think so. He's just this guy from school."

Mom narrowed her eyes at me, like she did when she suspected I was hiding things from her. I hated that face, because she was always right. "Does *he* have a name?" she asked.

"Yeah," I said. "Bradley. Didn't I say that?"

I hadn't. Mom knew it; I knew it. I scooped butter out of the tub and spread it across the muffin, wiping the excess from the knife on the edge.

Mom paused. "That's the boy who went to that dance with Haylee, isn't it?"

Whoops. I'd forgotten she knew that, but she'd driven us to the mall when we'd bought Haylee's dress. "Right," I said. "That's why we're getting together. Because he knew her too, you know? He's having a hard time."

Mom hesitated. I could sense the wheels turning. She wouldn't want to suggest to me that Haylee died because of Bradley, but she was thinking it. We were all thinking it.

"Where are you planning to go?" she asked.

That was a good thing about Mom. She liked to gather all the facts before laying down the law. It was probably all that practice she had at making recommendations to other people's parents. The downside was that once she made a decision, it wasn't easy to sway her otherwise.

"I don't know," I said. "We were going to talk about it when he gets here. It's not a real formal thing." Not a date. *Not a date.*

"Are his parents dropping him off?"

Now for the final blow. "No, he's going to pick me up in his car."

Mom sighed. "I don't know, Kira."

I gripped the edge of the counter. "Mom, please? Bradley really got the raw end after . . . you know. People at school think it's his fault. He needs someone to talk to."

Mom gave me a look.

I sighed. "I need to talk, too, you know?"

Her face softened. "Is he a safe driver?"

Bingo. "I wouldn't know. I've never been in the car with him before. I wouldn't do that without asking you first."

Mom smiled. Points for me.

I chewed my muffin, waiting for Mom to tell me she'd drive, or she'd come with us, or something equally embarrassing.

"You have to be home by dinner," she said. "And be sure you have your cell phone on. Call if you don't feel safe in the car with him."

I looked up from my muffin. "I can really go?"

Mom nodded reluctantly. "I'll need to know where you're going before you leave, and it needs to be a public place. But yes, you can go."

I didn't tell her about the things I'd seen Bradley and Fiona do in public places.

I was upstairs putting on my jeans when the doorbell rang. I looked at the clock. It was only eleven. Bradley shouldn't be showing up until noon.

Mom answered the door, and I waited at the top of the stairs, listening. Could I have gotten the time wrong?

I couldn't hear who was at the door, but I did hear Mom say, "Kira's upstairs. I'll go get her."

I glanced around. There were so many things I hadn't debated yet. Purse or no purse? Wallet? Keys?

Mom came to the bottom of the stairs and looked up at me. "Nick's here to see you," she said.

My pulse quickened. "Nick?"

"Nick. Haylee's cousin."

I rolled my eyes. "I know who he is. What does he want?"

Mom waved a dismissive hand at me. "I'm sure he'll tell you when you come downstairs." She walked off into the kitchen, where no doubt she would listen, just out of sight.

I ran downstairs and into the living room, and found Nick looking at my baby pictures, which Mom had lined up on the wall. He was holding a bouquet of daffodils in his hand.

Um, I thought. Why would Nick have brought me flowers? And right before Bradley showed up to take me out? He can't have come just to stare at my baby pictures.

"It's the curse of being the only child in a two-person family," I said.

Nick looked up at me. "What?"

I pointed to the wall of photos he'd been looking at. "The pictures are all me, all the time. I swear, I didn't hang them."

Nick laughed. "You were a cute kid."

My stomach squeezed. I was cute, but now I'm not? Or I was a kid, equally cute then and now? Or I'm still a kid, and just not as cute as I was?

I was a total freak. On that point I was clear.

I glanced down at the flowers. Nick lowered the flowers to his side, revealing the design on his shirt. This one was a picture of some kind of amorphous green blob creature holding a cannon. I didn't ask.

"I was just heading to Haylee's grave," he said quickly. "To take these to her. Do you want to come?"

Oh. Right. Of course the flowers weren't for me.

I thought about his offer. Me and Nick. Alone. I could text Bradley and tell him something came up.

But I needed to talk to him about Haylee. And with Christmas and New Year's and then school again, I didn't know when I'd get another chance. Besides, Nick and I wouldn't really be alone, would we? We'd be going to see Haylee. This was about her, not me.

Nick was the one thing in my life that still hadn't changed. "I can't," I said. "I already have . . . plans."

Nick nodded quickly. Maybe too quickly. "Sure," he said. "I figured you'd be busy, but I thought I'd check. Maybe some other time?"

"Yeah," I said, trying not to sound too eager. "Some other time, for sure."

Then we just stood there, nodding at each other. Nick turned to go.

"Wait," I said.

He looked back at me. Was I imagining it, or was that hope on his face?

No way. He was just being nice. Like always. "Maybe we could go tomorrow," I said. "I mean, if you want to go back that soon."

Nick stood by the front door, his hand on the doorknob. "Maybe Sunday?"

"Sure," I said. "Sunday works."

"Great. I'll come by and pick you up."

"Have fun at the cemetery," I said, like an idiot. "I mean—"

Nick gave me a sad smile. "I know what you mean," he said. "See you Sunday."

He opened the door and stepped out, shutting the door behind him.

I chewed on my lip. I had . . . still not a date . . . *plans* with Nick.

And with Bradley.

If ever there was a moment when I needed to call Haylee to sort things out, this was it.

At noon I went into the bathroom, ran a brush through my hair, and made sure I didn't have anything awkward stuck in my teeth. 12:02. I found a beige purse and stuffed my wallet and keys into it, then debated about whether it clashed with my sweater. 12:04. I picked up a magazine and read half an article about spring fashions. 12:07. I listened to thirty seconds of a song on the radio before I got sick of the lyrics. 12:09. I picked up some laundry and made my bed. 12:17. I was about to pull out some homework when the doorbell rang again.

I ran down the stairs, but Mom got there before I even reached the living room. I should have been stalling closer to the door. She must have been lying in wait.

"Hello," I could hear her say. "I'm Kira's mother, Ms. Turner."

Ugh. She always made Haylee call her that, too, in a jab about how inappropriate it was that Aaron told me to call him and Hazel by their first names. *Please*, I thought. *Please don't let her say anything too embarrassing.*

65

I ran around the corner just as Bradley stepped inside. He had his hair slicked back, and wore a polo shirt and dark, dark jeans—the kind that probably bled in the wash. He shook Mom's hand. "I'm Bradley," he said. "Nice to meet you."

He looked her straight in the eye, and I saw her shoulders relax a bit.

"Okay, I'm ready," I said, more to Mom than to Bradley. "See you later."

Mom raised her eyebrows at me over her shoulder.

Right. We had to pick a public place.

Mom put a hand on her hip. "Kira says you have your license."

Ugh. Could we not grill him like a flayed fish? "Mom," I said.

But Bradley nodded eagerly. "Yeah. I've had it for six months. I'm a really good driver. I've never been in an accident."

Mom did not look comforted. I guessed six months wasn't as big a sample size as she would have liked. "Where will you two be going?"

"I was thinking we could go to the arcade at Golfland." He glanced at me. "They have some batting cages."

I nodded. That was the kind of activity Mom was looking for. "I think I have some quarters upstairs."

Mom followed me up the stairs, rather than cornering Bradley. I could hear her rattling around in the change jar in her office.

I opened my desk drawer and scooped out some coins. Mom appeared in my doorway holding some change. "I'll be home all day," she said. "You have your phone? It's charged?"

"Got it," I said.

"Call if you need me to pick you up."

"Thanks." I took the change and headed for the door before she could change her mind.

The car Bradley was driving was a slick, shiny stick shift. I was reasonably sure it was a sports car of some kind, but beyond that I was clueless.

Bradley unlocked the passenger door for me, and I climbed in. The car smelled like new leather.

"Did you pick Haylee up for the dance in this?" I asked as Bradley climbed into the driver's seat.

"Yeah," he said. "It's awesome, huh? Didn't she tell you about it?"

I dug my nails into my palm. Of course. He probably thought I'd heard all about it. Haylee lived for a whole weekend after the dance. She should have called me. She should have told me everything. "We didn't talk," I said. "You saw her more recently than I did."

Bradley paused with his keys in the ignition. He reached his hand over and placed it gently on top of my wrist, which hadn't felt awkward on top of my knee until that moment. I tried not to move. I tried not to breathe.

What was he doing?

"I'm sorry," he said. "I bet everyone's bugging you to talk about her. We don't have to if you don't want to."

Then he moved his hand from my wrist, and turned the key. The engine roared to a start.

I did want to talk about Haylee. She was *all* I wanted to talk about. Did that mean he didn't want me to bother *him* about it? I couldn't exactly follow that up by peppering him with questions, which was the whole reason I was here.

But if he didn't want to talk about it, why was he here?

"Okay," I said.

I fiddled with my arm rest. What else would I talk to Bradley about? Baseball? There wasn't a lot to say about that since the season hadn't started yet.

No. We were here to talk about Haylee, and that's what I had to do, even if I offended him.

"Actually," I said, "I had some questions for you. Is that okay?"

Bradley raised his eyebrows, but he nodded. "Sure. Fine. Whatever you want."

I tried to reconcile this new, accommodating Bradley with the guy who defiled my locker. Though, I guess he did move when I asked him to. I had to give him that.

Bradley drove to the edge of my neighborhood and waited to

turn right onto the first major street. He didn't look at me, but his fingers tapped the steering wheel. Waiting.

I wasn't sure how to begin. This wasn't like getting the story from Haylee, where I could have just sat her down and said, *spill.*

I finally settled on, "Did you have fun at the dance?"

Bradley ran a hand through his hair. "I guess," he said.

I chewed on my lower lip. The way he said that was pretty dismissive. Obviously he didn't want to talk about it. I was as bad as my mother, trying to drag information out of him that he didn't want to give. He'd had to talk to the *police*, for goodness' sake. Hadn't he been through enough?

I should have gone to the cemetery with Nick.

Then Bradley said, "*I* thought we had fun."

"Really?"

"Yeah. I mean, Haylee's kind of quiet, you know? But once she loosens up, she's a lot of fun."

"Huh," I said. I bit my lip. I shouldn't have sounded that incredulous out loud. It wasn't that Haylee wasn't fun. She was. When it was just her and me, and no one else around who would make her self-conscious.

I ran my hands over the smooth leather seats, trying to imagine Haylee sitting where I was, talking to Bradley, laughing, being *fun.*

It wasn't coming.

"What about you?" Bradley asked. "You miss her, yeah?"

Of course I missed her. But I hadn't spent the last few years acting like I didn't know she existed. What right did Bradley have to think she was fun? He couldn't know. Could he?

I'd been quiet for too long.

"Hey," Bradley said. "I told you we didn't have to talk about it."

I squirmed. If we weren't going to talk about his date with Haylee, what was I doing here?

The batting cages smelled like motor oil and new rubber. We shared a machine, taking turns, though Bradley hit twice as many balls as I did. I'd never been the best batter on the team. It was my pitching that kept me in the line up.

Bradley started coaching me on my form on our third swap. "Choke up on the bat," he said.

I *was* choked up, but he stepped right up behind me, putting his arms on either side of me, and his hands over mine. He gently slipped the bat between my fingers, his body pressing against me from behind.

My heart pounded so hard I was sure Bradley could feel it through my spine.

What was he *doing*?

"Like this," he said, patting the bat firmly.

I gritted my teeth. As if no one had ever taught me to hold a bat before. As if I hadn't been playing for seven years.

"I'm thirsty," I said, turning and stepping to the side. Bradley took the hint and dropped his arms, letting me put some space between me and him. "Want a Coke?"

He nodded. "Sure."

I fed my quarters into the vending machine and came up with enough for two sodas and a bag of Doritos. I found a bench next to the pink plywood windmill where the families filed past to get to the first hole. Bradley sat down next to me and I handed him one of the Coke cans. He popped it open and then extended his arm along the back of the bench behind me, so that his fingers brushed my forearm on the far side.

My skin tingled where his fingers touched it. I leaned away ever so slightly, breaking contact between his fingers and my arm, but they nudged back again. Goosebumps broke out down my arm.

Focus, I thought. This was about Haylee. That's why I was here. "So did you and Haylee dance a lot?"

Bradley shrugged. "Yeah," he said. "It was a dance, you know."

"Dancing in front of people usually made Haylee nervous," I said.

"Yeah, well," Bradley said, "is *anyone* really comfortable at those things?"

I'd have thought Bradley Johansen would be comfortable anywhere.

Bradley took a long drag of his Coke. "She seemed fine to me, but maybe I didn't know her well enough to tell the difference."

There it was. My opening. "Tell me more about it. Maybe the details will mean something to me, even if they didn't to you."

Bradley squeezed my shoulder. He was like the anti-Nick, touching me when there was no reason to. "Okay," he said. "Ask whatever you want."

Down to business. "Tell me about your date," I said. "Tell me everything."

"Like what? We went to the dance. We danced."

I sighed. "Start with when you went to pick her up. Tell me about that."

"I picked her up in my car. My dad bought it a couple days before, so she was the first girl I got to pick up in it."

I'm sure Fiona loved that. "So the car is actually yours?"

Bradley grinned. "As long as I keep my grades up."

I didn't know anyone else from school who owned a car. Nick was the only upperclassman I was friends with, and he drove his mom's. "And then what?"

"We met up with some people at Ruben's house and hung out for a while before we went to the dance."

Ruben Hernandez was the shortstop for the boys varsity baseball team. He was a junior—the same age as Nick—and his parents lived in a huge house in a neighborhood up on the hill. I'd never been there, but he hosted a lot of parties—I guess his parents were out of town a lot.

"How long were you there?"

"I don't know, an hour? Long enough to get some drinks, and to help get stuff ready for the after party."

"Drinks, like, alcohol?" I cringed at how surprised I sounded. But if Bradley thought I was naive, he didn't show it. "Sure.

We both had a couple."

My dad was a drunk, which is why he and Mom never got married, and why I don't even know who he is. But Mom says it's genetic, and the only way to be sure I don't turn out like him is not to drink. Not that I mind. Beer smells like fermented body odor mixed with cat urine.

But I knew Haylee drank sometimes when I wasn't around. It would explain why Haylee was cool with the dancing.

For a moment, my mind raced. Maybe the alcohol mixed with her anti-depressants. Maybe she hadn't meant to kill herself, she'd just died of the bad combination.

But she'd died on Sunday night, not Friday. That was too long for a drug interaction. Wasn't it?

"Were you drunk?"

"Not *drunk* drunk. I could still drive just fine."

Great. If my mother heard that, she'd never let me in the car with him again, and I'd hardly be able to blame her.

"So," I said, "did you, you know, kiss her?"

Bradley withdrew his arm, planting his elbows on his knees. "Jeez, Kira."

"What?" I asked. "Is that too personal?"

"It's kind of grotesque," he said, "talking about kissing a dead girl. Besides, isn't it wrong to kiss and tell?"

The guy whose tongue I'd seen inside Fiona's mouth at every possible angle was suddenly shy about kissing. "Sorry," I said.

Maybe Haylee had been different for him. Maybe he thought she was special. He *better* have, because if he treated her like Fiona, I'd kick him in the balls.

Either way, I couldn't exactly fault him for being careful with her memory.

Now the big question. The one I'd been asking myself for weeks. "Why'd you ask her out in the first place?"

Bradley leaned his head back, looking up at the spinning blades of the windmill. "What do you mean?"

"She doesn't seem like your type."

71

He gave me half a smile. "And what, exactly, is my type?"

"Um," I said. "Fiona?"

Bradley laughed. "Maybe I was looking for something different."

Couldn't blame him for that.

"Look," Bradley said, "this is way worse for you than it is for me. I went out with her once. You guys were like joined at the hip."

When Haylee was alive, that comment would have made me crazy. We were separate people, after all. But now, I guessed we were a little bit joined.

"Come on," Bradley said, grabbing me by one of my hands and lifting me to my feet. Once I was standing, he held onto my hand longer than he needed to, pulling me toward the car. "I better get you home before your mother freaks out."

We hadn't been out that long. Mom was probably fine. But I let him lead me toward the car. I'd done what I came for, hadn't I?

But what about Bradley? What did *he* want?

Bradley drove me home, obeying the speed limit and stopping for stop signs and traffic lights. At least when he was sober, he actually was a decent driver.

He parked in front of my house and stretched his arm across the back of my seat, not touching me this time, but still hanging there, like he might at any time. I already had my fingers on the door handle. As I opened the door, Bradley said, "Did you hear about Catherine's party?"

"No," I said. Catherine Kandinsky was on the softball team with me, and she had English with Bradley, Haylee, and me. But we were softball friends, not hang-out friends.

"It's tomorrow night," he said. "Open invitation. So maybe I'll see you there?"

See me? There? Open party probably meant no parents, and lots of booze. Mom would definitely not be up for that.

"I don't know," I said.

"Because I'd like to. See you again, I mean."

He smiled with his whole face, his eyes crinkling. A cold rush washed over me. I looked at Bradley, wide eyed. And for a moment, I saw what Haylee used to see in him: His eyes were so blue that I felt like I could fall into them. And he sat in my driveway, telling me he wanted to see me again.

I thought about what he'd said earlier, about wanting something different than Fiona. And in that moment, I wanted to say yes. He might be Haylee's crush, but he was also a guy, paying attention to me, touching me, wanting to spend time with me.

"Yeah," I said. "I'll be there."

Bradley waved as I closed the door, then waited for me to get in the front door before he sped off down the street.

I leaned against the front door, looking at the place in the living room where Nick had stood just hours before.

Two boys inviting me places in one day. And for one of them, it didn't seem to be all about Haylee.

Seven Months Before

In the last weeks of our freshman year, a rash of parties broke out. The seniors threw parties because they were graduating. The juniors celebrated because they were about to be seniors. The sophomores shadowed whichever upper-classmen they could attach themselves to, and the freshmen crashed when they could, thrilled that soon someone else would be the butt of the freshmen jokes.

But for the most part, I missed the scene entirely. Official softball season was over, but tournament season was just beginning, which meant I was off every weekend with Aaron and the tournament team.

I was free over Memorial Day weekend, though, and I spent all week prepping Haylee to crash Crystal Castro's party.

"Crystal's a sophomore," I told Haylee. "It won't be that crazy, or that big."

"It's just going to be a bunch of people getting drunk," Haylee said. "Why would you want to go?"

I shrugged. "Maybe it'll be funny to watch?"

Haylee eyed me warily. "Why don't you just go with your softball friends?" she asked.

"They're coming too," I said. "We can all ride over together."

Haylee rolled her eyes. She didn't like to hang out with my

friends from the team, because she said all we talked about was sports. That wasn't entirely true—we also talked about boys—but that point never seemed to comfort Haylee.

"Fine," she said. "But I don't want to ride over with your friends. I'll walk."

"You might get there before us," I said.

"Yeah, so?"

"So I don't want you to be uncomfortable—"

She turned on me. "You're gone a lot, you know? And somehow I manage to breathe in and out all weekend long."

"Sorry," I said. "Obviously you can handle it."

Haylee slammed her locker closed. "And I don't need you to hold my hand."

"Noted," I said. "But you better show up."

Haylee didn't respond.

The night of the party, though, I ran a fever. My heartbeat pounded in my head. Mom took one look at me and sent me to bed.

"I'm meeting Haylee," I said.

"Call and cancel," Mom said. "You're not going anywhere."

Haylee didn't answer my texts, so I called her, but she didn't pick up. She wouldn't answer my phone calls for the rest of the weekend, and I kept picturing her hiding in a closet at the party, waiting to hear my voice so that she could come out. At school on Tuesday, I expected her to freak out at me, or pointedly ignore me, but when I caught her in the hall before first period, she just smiled. "Sorry you missed the party," she said. "I had a couple beers. Do you hate me?"

"Don't be stupid. You went without me?"

"Yeah," Haylee said. "You made me promise to show. It wasn't as bad as I thought it would be. A bunch of juniors showed up. One of them vomited all over Crystal's mom's velvet love seat, and he tried to clean it up with a cup of water that turned out to be orange soda. It was kinda hilarious."

I blinked at her.

She shrugged. "Maybe you had to be there."

I nodded. "You had fun?"

Haylee opened her locker and put a hand on her hip. "What? I'm not allowed to do that without you?"

"No, I mean—"

"It was awesome, actually. The beer tasted awful, but after the first one I stopped feeling stupid when I spoke, and I stopped worrying that everyone was staring at me. Or maybe they just stare less when they're drunk. I don't know."

"That's great," I said. "And you found people to talk to?"

"Not really people," Haylee said, shrugging.

Oh no. A cat? A dog? Crystal's pet goldfish?

Haylee flipped through her textbooks like nothing was out of the ordinary. "Jody Nguyen's cousin was there. He goes to SCU, you know?"

I didn't. "Oh?"

"And he hung out with me all night. Just me and him, chilling on the couch."

Haylee. Chilling with a college guy. "All night?"

"Sure," she said. "Well, until Crystal's uncle came by to check on her. Then we all had to clear out, so Wex drove me home."

"Wex?" I asked.

"That's what he goes by. It's short for something, but I don't remember what."

Wow. "Did your parents get mad?"

"Nah," Haylee said. "They weren't waiting up for me. I told them I was sleeping over at your house."

As she should have. If I'd known she was going to talk to a guy all by herself, I would have suggested it. "So do you think Wex is into you?"

Haylee shrugged. "Probably not. I mean, he's a college guy. They play by different rules, you know? He's probably forgotten me already."

"So nothing happened."

She gave me a look. "A lot of things happened, actually. I

76

think I just told you about them."

I paused. She was dodging the question intentionally, to make me fish.

"Come on," I said. "Tell me what I missed."

"Not much," Haylee said. "Really. You wouldn't have liked the party. Everyone was drunk. Even me."

She brushed her hair out of her face, and I saw a fresh red line snaking down her wrist. This was a long one—three or four inches at least.

That's when I stopped pushing. Haylee might be giving me a happier version of the story than what actually happened, but if that's the story she needed to be okay, I wasn't going to be the one to take it from her.

Chapter Seven

I told Mom that Catherine's parents were going to be at the party, and thankfully she didn't call to check. And because Mom knew Catherine from my team, I didn't even have to mention that it was Bradley who'd asked me to come.

It took me an hour to decide what to wear. I avoided the issue at first, taking a shower to shave the cactus spines off my legs, and then stood in front of my closet, considering.

Normally if I was hanging out with a guy, I'd call Haylee to talk about wardrobe choices. Instead, I tried on half my wardrobe and finally settled on a pair of skinny jeans and a red, fitted sweater. I put on lipstick and French-braided my hair. Haylee had taught me how to do it myself by propping my elbows up on the headboard of my bed for support, but if she'd been there to do it for me, it would have looked classier. Then I went into the bathroom to look at myself in the full-length mirror.

Clearly I was trying too hard. Also, the braid puffed out over my ears, instead of lying down flat. I undid my hair and pulled it into a ponytail. Much more casual. Then I rubbed off half my makeup.

I stood, staring at myself in the mirror.

My neck prickled. The place behind me in the mirror was blank—nothing there but floor tiles and a fluffy pink towel.

But I felt her all the same—Haylee's ghost. *What are you doing, Kira?* she asked. *Do you* like *him?*

"Of course not," I whispered to her.

I could feel Haylee's smirk even though I couldn't see her. She wasn't sure about that.

Neither was I.

I opened the bathroom door and rushed out, shutting myself back in my room, hoping she couldn't float through walls. If the real Haylee were here, I knew exactly what she'd say. She'd want me to go hang out with Bradley so she could savor every detail when I got home. She'd consider it dating-by-proxy. My hanging out with Bradley was the next best thing to seeing him herself.

So I wasn't betraying her. I wasn't.

If only I could convince her ghost of that.

I left for the party after dark. Mom offered me a ride, but Catherine only lived six blocks away, and I didn't need Mom witnessing the total parental lack, so I told her I'd walk. I ducked out before she decided to give me a serious talk about rape safety or teen drug use.

When I got to Catherine's, I could hear the bass from the street. Stephanie Nye sat in the window seat with her back to me, leaning over so far that I could see her butt crack. The front door had a note saying to come in, probably because they couldn't hear the doorbell over the music.

I opened the door and wandered through the entryway toward the living room. I could hear people talking over the music, which at this volume meant the house had to be packed. In the living room, groups clustered around chairs, a few people sitting on them and the rest on the floor at their feet. Lexa Io draped herself over the back of a couch with her breasts hanging in Greg Anzano's face.

I was really surprised to see not only Stephanie but Fiona Gil and a couple other popular girls. Catherine was cool, but she was more of a floater, drifting between circles. That put her a lot higher on the popularity scale than someone like me, but not high enough to be really popular, like Stephanie and Fiona were.

Katie from the softball team leaned against the far wall with some other girls. She waved at me and I waved back like we were friends, but she was the one who had called me a dyke last season, so I wasn't eager to hang out.

Fiona and Stephanie were staring at me. Fiona leaned over to Steph—whose skirt couldn't have been more than eight inches long—and said something in her ear. I could imagine what she was saying: how can she be here when her best friend just died? Katie was staring at me, too, like I was some exhibit at a zoo. Next on our tour, Kira Turner, who recently lost her best friend. Any time now we should see tears; those are a normal stage of the grieving process.

Ugh. I was being just like Haylee, thinking everyone was talking about me because of Haylee's death, when they were probably just making fun of my outfit. Most people had stopped staring at me by now, but I was still standing awkwardly in the hall. Spencer Mann came up behind me and pulled me into the living room. He turned to me and opened his big mouth. The music was so loud in here that I was amazed I could hear him.

"Hey, Kira, glad you could make it. Have a seat." He was using his radio voice—the one he used when he wanted to hold the attention of the entire room, which for Spencer was practically all the time. He sat down next to Fiona, who looked at him like he was barely tolerable.

Stephanie pawed Spencer's arm. Every statement she made came out like a question. "I still can't believe you didn't bring the beer?" she said. "You so totally fail?"

"Hey, who made it my job?" Spencer asked. "I'm here to provide the entertainment!"

Stephanie rolled her eyes. "I said you were the beer man? You said it was no problem?"

I leaned in, trying to get into the conversation, but Fiona glared at me before I could open my mouth.

"Didn't your friend just die?" she asked.

The only way to shut Fiona up was to be as far in her face as she was in mine. I stared her right in the eyes. "She's the one who's dead," I said. "Not me."

Fiona's eyebrows shot up. She'd drawn one on darker than the other.

And she actually looked impressed.

"Hey, where's your boyfriend, Fiona?" Spencer asked.

Stephanie rolled her eyes "You mean her totally ex-boyfriend?"

"Shut up," Fiona said. I could tell by the look on her face that in her mind, he wasn't *totally* ex. I could bet she didn't know I'd gone out with Bradley the day before, and I wasn't going to be the one to tell her.

At that point I was sure I'd made the wrong decision about coming to the party. I should have walked out the door when I had the chance. If I went to the bathroom and climbed out the window, would anyone even notice I'd gone?

Then Bradley walked in the front door. My stomach fluttered. *Jeez, Kira*, I thought. *He'll probably ignore you. He probably just asked you out of pity.*

Fiona watched Bradley even closer than I did. She leaned forward in her chair and squeezed her shoulders together, so her breasts practically popped out of her tube top. I seriously thought Spencer was going to wet himself, but instead he crossed an arm over his crotch.

Bradley walked right over to our group, but he was looking at me, not Fiona. The fluttering in my stomach turned into a frantic crawl, and I wondered if some anxiety monster was going to crawl out of my chest like in that movie with the alien.

Bradley shouted at Spencer over the music: "Hey man, scoot down."

Away from me. He meant scoot down away from me.

He hadn't forgotten me.

Spencer moved over immediately, without complaint, and I moved slightly to my left so that Bradley could sit down between us. Bradley's thigh pressed up against mine, and Fiona gave me a look of death. Maybe *she* was the one who was going to sprout the alien. No doubt it would devour me on the spot.

Spencer turned to Bradley and said, "What's up?" He used a genuine tone with Bradley, because Bradley was so much more popular.

"Not much," Bradley shouted, putting his arm around my shoulders and squeezing me closer to him. I hadn't really expected that. I could feel both Fiona and Stephanie glaring, so I tried to avoid looking at them.

Catherine came around the corner. Her blond hair cascaded in tight, frizzy curls down her back. During softball season, she always kept it pulled up. She looked straight at me and skipped over to the stereo, turning it down. The subwoofer on the floor still pounded with the beat, but my ears rang a little with the sudden decrease in noise. "Kira!" she shouted. "You made it!"

Catherine hadn't ever looked so happy to see me in my life. She didn't seem to remember that she hadn't invited me. Did she feel sorry for me?

But then she sat down on the arm of the couch and gave Bradley this big, toothy smile.

No. She wasn't even thinking me. She was eyeing the guy with his arm around me. And somehow, inexplicably, some impulse in my gut shouted *mine*.

Bradley returned Catherine's smile. "Hey," he said. "Nice house."

"Thanks," Catherine said, as if she could take credit for it.

Now Stephanie turned her glare on Catherine, and Fiona stood and stalked off.

I couldn't say I was sad about that.

"So, have you started training for the season yet?" Catherine asked me.

I shrugged. "Sort of." One night of pitching didn't really amount to training, but I wasn't going to announce that I'd done nothing in front of Bradley.

Bradley smirked. "Yeah, you two better start early. The softball team needs as much practice as they can get."

"We could beat you any day," Catherine said.

"Please. You throw like a bunch of girls."

"We are a bunch of girls," I said. "So?"

Bradley had this wide grin, and he glanced in the direction Fiona had gone and started rubbing my arm.

Oh, no. Was this all about her? Had this always been all about her?

Catherine laughed. "Yeah, really. You wouldn't have a chance against us."

Mr. Varsity Freshman could probably play in circles around both of us, but I wasn't going to come to his defense.

Catherine started jabbering away to Bradley about playing first base, since they had that position in common. Stephanie got up to join Fiona in the hall. I could see the two of them glaring at me from the edge of my vision, but I wasn't going to give them the satisfaction of noticing they were there.

Bradley's hand felt like it was starting to wear the skin off my arm, since he was still rubbing the same spot. And then he said in my ear, "Do you think it's hot in here?"

I did, but I wasn't sure it had anything to do with the room. So I said, "Yeah, I guess."

And he said, a little louder but still clearly to me, "Let's go outside for a while."

The room got hotter.

I knew I shouldn't go. But I wanted out of there, away from Fiona and Stephanie, and Catherine, and the unrelenting beat of the music, which matched a growing pounding in my head. I *did* want to go outside.

So I said, "Okay."

Bradley smiled.

I looked down at Catherine as we stood up. "We'll be back in a little while," I said.

Catherine looked confused, and maybe a little bit hurt, but I stepped right by her and headed for the door. Bradley followed me, and when I turned around to look at him he was turned around looking at Fiona, who was glaring like a rabid cat, fangs and all.

Bradley grabbed the door for me, which was really awkward since he was standing behind me and had to reach across me. We stepped out into the night.

No one had turned on the porch light, and the sky was overcast and dark. Here we were. Me and Bradley. Alone, with only the still-audible beat pulsing behind us.

My heart beat overtime to match. "Did you want to come out here to talk about Haylee?" I asked.

He shook his head, and reached his hand under my elbow, guiding me closer to him. "Not unless there was something else you wanted to say."

Every thought whisked out of my mind, and I couldn't think of a single thing. And that's when I knew for sure that I wasn't there for Haylee anymore.

Bradley steered me toward the shadowed porch swing. A breeze blew across the front of the house, and I shivered.

Bradley ran a hand up and down my arm, which sprouted goosebumps, more from his touch than from the wind.

"Hey, are you cold?" Bradley asked.

"A little," I said.

I expected him to give me his windbreaker, but instead he pulled me into him. We stood under the canopy of the swing, with the seat brushing our knees as it swayed with the wind. Bradley wrapped my arms around his waist, which felt taut under his T-shirt. Our stomachs pressed together, and he zipped his jacket against my back, so it held us together.

He had to be able to feel my heartbeat. I couldn't feel his over the pounding of mine. Wrapped in that way, my forehead rested naturally against his collarbone. My body knew how to fold against him, even if my brain was ringing five alarms telling me to get out of there.

"You'll warm up in a second," he said.

Did that mean he intended to let me go after that? No. It was a line. One he might have used on Fiona, or Haylee before me.

The pounding in my head faded into a fuzz, and I couldn't think of anything except the way Bradley's arms snaked around my waist, toying with the back of the waistband on my jeans. I'd listened to a thousand of Haylee's fantasies about those arms. But never, never had I put myself inside them.

I looked up at him to tell him to unzip the jacket, so I could get away from his warm body and think again, but when I did, Bradley's face moved closer and I realized that he was going to kiss me.

Words finally came to me: I'm not Haylee. But his lips were on mine before I could say it.

His mouth felt warm and uncomfortably wet, and his nose exhaled hot breath down my face and onto my neck. My goosebumps spread over my body, until every follicle stood erect.

I wondered if I could reach around and unzip his jacket from the back. But then a voice hissed from deep in the back of my brain: Don't be stupid. A boy is kissing you. *You.* So I tried to match the movements of Bradley's lips, but our mouths tangled together, off balance.

The flip-flopping of my stomach dropped several inches. He must know I had no idea what I was doing. Suddenly, the synchronized tonguings I'd seen him perform with Fiona seemed a lot more impressive—like an Olympic sport. As if on cue, Bradley shoved his tongue past my flailing lips and into my mouth. I could taste stale Doritos in his teeth.

The jacket pinned my elbows to his sides, cutting off my circulation. I slid my hands up inside the jacket and rested them on his shoulders so they stuck out like a chicken. Bradley's slobbering encompassed my chin, and I leaned my head away instinctively, tightening the collar of the jacket around both of our necks.

I squirmed. Bradley seemed to get the hint. He shifted toward the porch swing, pulling me with him. "Turn around," he said, sliding me around in the jacket and then sitting down on the swing, so I ended up sitting on his lap with his arms around me. The collar of the jacket was choking me a little, so I unzipped it a few inches. But I guess he didn't really get the hint, because he moved his face next to mine and kissed my cheek, migrating a little toward my ear. I felt his hands moving up inside the jacket toward my breasts, so I squeezed with my arms, trying to keep his hands down without him noticing I was doing it on purpose.

And then he scooted me farther up his lap, and I finally unzipped the jacket, fumbling with the bottom of the clasp. When I stood up, Bradley stood with me. My hands were shaking. I hoped he couldn't see that in the dark.

What was wrong with me? A boy finally kissed me, and now I was freaking out? But I thought kissing would be different—more romantic. I thought it would make me feel closer to him, not squirmy inside.

Bradley opened his mouth to say something, but the front door opened. Catherine stepped out onto the porch and I edged further away from Bradley. Too quickly. Her eyes got all wide and I wondered if she knew we'd been kissing. Was the slobber visible? I forced myself not to wipe my face.

"Hey," she said. "We're going to play some games if you guys want to come back inside."

Games. Like spin the bottle? I had to get out of here.

Bradley nodded at her. "We'll be right there." She looked at us for a second until she got the hint and went back in.

"I guess you better go back," I said to Bradley, after she was gone.

"You're not coming?"

I edged so far from him that I had to step down off the side of the porch, smashing some groundcover as I went. "No," I said. "I just want to go home."

"You sure?" Bradley asked.

"Yeah. You stay, though," I said. "I'll see you later."

"Sure," Bradley said, heading toward the door. "Later."

Then he went inside, just like that.

I stood in Catherine's foliage, alone in the dark. My hands were still trembling, so I shoved them deep into my pockets.

That, I said to myself, *was supremely uncool.* What must Bradley think of me? He must think I was a total spaz, that's what. I mean, kissing was supposed to be fun, wasn't it? He certainly seemed to have fun doing it with Fiona, so if there was a problem between the two of us, there was a good bet it was me.

Someone bumped into the door from the inside, and I heard laughter over the music. I backed onto Catherine's lawn, and turned and walked down to the sidewalk. I couldn't help thinking that Nick wouldn't have left me alone in the dark.

Nick wouldn't have kissed me, either.

I should have gone home, but instead I walked by Haylee's. I knew I couldn't go in, so I just stood on the sidewalk, looking up at Haylee's tree—a massive, gangly thing that shadowed the house from the street. Her mother hated it, but Haylee and Aaron both forbade her to call a tree-remover. It was the only thing they agreed on, and I was pretty sure that's why she let them have their way.

I stood on the sidewalk, holding my breath, looking for Haylee's ghost. I waited for the hairs to rise on the back of my neck, for the goosebumps I'd felt with Bradley to return. But if Haylee was there, she didn't make her presence known. I couldn't feel her watching me.

Maybe she'd given up on me. After what I'd done tonight, maybe she ought to.

As I looked up at Haylee's dark window, I wished I could take this memory of kissing Bradley and hand it over to her. I'd only called Bradley for her sake, after all. I never would have gone after him on my own. I wondered if she'd had a kiss just like that with him, if it had been painful and awkward, and made her want to die, because being with him wasn't what she'd thought it would be.

As I turned to walk home, I wanted to take one more detour,

to walk by Nick's house, but I didn't. Haylee couldn't look out and see me, couldn't wonder why I was there. Nick could. And seeing him tonight would be too much. What if, in some bizarre moment of insanity, he decided to kiss me, too? Would he be able to taste Bradley on my lips, like a stale Dorito?

If kissing Nick was going to be as awkward as kissing Bradley, I'd pass.

Sometimes reality couldn't measure up to the dream.

Two Years Before

Our last New Year's in middle school, Haylee and I holed up in her room with her dad's little TV from the garage and a mountain of junk food.

After the ball dropped, we were sitting on her bed in our pajamas, splitting a tray of mozzarella sticks.

Haylee leaned back on her bed and propped her foot up on her knee. "So it's official," she said. "I'm a crazy person."

"Is this supposed to be news?" I asked.

She threw a pillow at my head. Then she hopped up and went into the bathroom across the hall, and came back with a yellow prescription bottle.

"Happy pills," she said. Then she mimicked a stiff, official voice. "For depression and anxiety."

"Your therapist gave you those?"

"No," Haylee said. "An official doctor. Shrink. Person."

I didn't know she'd been seeing more doctors. "Have you started them?"

"Two weeks ago," Haylee said, shaking the bottle so the pills rattled inside.

"And you're just telling me this now?"

"Yeah." She cringed. "Don't say anything in front of my mother. She said if I told people, they'd think I was nuts."

"I'm already aware," I said.

Haylee smiled. "I know, right? But she told Aunt Julie about it and Aunt Julie thinks the drugs will wipe out my emotions and turn me into a zombie." She rolled her eyes back into her head and ambled back to the bed, moaning.

I laughed. "So do they?"

"No," Haylee said. "I don't think they do anything, actually. I'm as crazy as ever."

"So they're not-quite-happy pills."

"Oh, no," Haylee said. "They're happy pills all right. They make my *mother* happy."

Chapter Eight

On Sunday, Nick and I had the cemetery to ourselves—unless you counted Haylee and her new roommates.

I'd hated being here during Haylee's burial. Today felt different—peaceful. I sat cross-legged on the grass, looking at Haylee's grave. I'd expected it to be covered in bare dirt, since it was new, but the cemetery people had laid a grid of sod squares over the top. Haylee's headstone hadn't been put in yet, so the plot wasn't marked. A concrete pad sat where the stone would go when it was finished. She was buried next to her grandmother and grandfather, Leonard and Helen Ricks.

They'd both died old.

Nick leaned over the grave, careful not to touch the new grass, and pulled wilted daffodils out of the jar on the concrete marker, replacing them with the fresh ones he'd brought. Then he sat down next to me, leaning back on his palms. Today his shirt featured famous members of the Communist party, only they were throwing a literal party, with balloons and confetti.

"Where'd you get daffodils in December?" I asked.

"The flower shop," he said.

They must have been planted under grow-lights somewhere, tricked into blooming in the wrong season.

On top of the concrete pad someone had left a card with that lame footprints poem on the front of it. The one that ends:

And the Lord replied
My child, I would never leave you.
When you saw only one set of footprints
It was then that I carried you.

I didn't see Jesus showing up to carry me today. I picked the poem up. "I'm throwing this away," I said.

"Nah," Nick said, reaching over and taking it out of my hands. He pulled a pen from his pocket and crossed out the last line of the poem, scrawling something underneath.

When he handed it back to me it read:

~~*It was then that I carried you*~~
It was then that we walked single file to hide our numbers.

I smiled, and nestled the card back on the grave. A cold breeze blew through, and I shivered, running my hands up my sleeves.

Nick looked at me. "You want my jacket?"

I thought of pressing against Bradley, zipped inside his windbreaker. I could feel myself blush.

"No, I'm okay." It felt right to be cold in a graveyard. Everybody else was.

Nick stretched his legs out. "Thanks for coming with me."

I still wasn't sure why he'd asked me to come. Was he just being friendly?

I could still feel Bradley's mouth on mine. Just thinking about it made me want to wipe my face with the back of my hand. Nick didn't seem to notice. And why would he? I was just his cousin's little friend.

Nick smiled at me, and my heart missed a beat.

Ugh. I might not know why Bradley wanted to kiss me, but at least I could tell *what* he wanted.

"You know what I miss about Haylee?" Nick asked.

"What?"

"The way she always stole my food," he said. "Anytime I had

a candy bar or a bag of chips, she'd take half of it, without even asking. Isn't that a stupid thing to miss?"

"Nah," I said.

"It drove me crazy when she did that. But now every time I eat something, I want to leave half of it behind."

"She knew it drove you nuts," I said. "That's why she did it."

He laughed. "What do you miss?"

A million things. "I miss having someone to talk to," I said.

Nick was quiet. "I know it's not the same," he said. "But you can talk to me."

Maybe about some things, but not about Bradley. "Have you come here a lot?" I asked.

"This is the third time. I didn't see her as much as you did. So it wouldn't have been that strange for me not to see her for this long, you know? That's why I come here. To remind myself that it's real."

"I thought I was the only one who didn't want to forget." Sitting here, remembering, felt right. It should matter enough to feel real.

It should matter enough to cry about, too.

Nick shook his head. "If I forget, then it sneaks up on me all at once. Remembering after forgetting is worse than remembering all the time."

"Like spreading the pain out is better than dealing with it all in one dose."

Nick looked down at his hands. "When you say it that way, it sounds crazy."

I smiled. "It's not crazy," I said. "Not any crazier than feeling guilty for forgetting."

Nick looked at me. "You feel guilty?"

"Yeah," I said. "My best friend just died. I should be sad all the time."

He tore up a piece of grass and twiddled it between his fingers. "Don't cause yourself more pain intentionally. There's too much of that going around."

I picked at the grass in front of me. "I still don't get why she did it."

Nick shook his head. "She was going through one of her low times, I guess."

"She'd done that before. A lot."

Nick shrugged. "It's a medical problem. Sometimes those get worse."

"So something goes wrong in your brain and kills you?" I asked. "How can that happen?" Sure, she got depressed. She hid in her room; she cried on the phone. But those times never lasted for long. And then Haylee would be back. "Do you know how she did it?"

He drew a deep breath. "Yeah, pills. Her dad's pain meds and her anti-depressants, plus whatever else she could find."

In my mind, I saw Haylee lying back and falling asleep, her spirit floating out of her body, no longer weighed down by the endless highs and lows.

"I read online that pills don't work all the time," Nick said. "Most of the time the person will throw up, maybe ruin their stomach lining for life, but they'll survive."

"But not Haylee," I said.

He shook his head. "No. Not Haylee."

"Do you know who found her?"

Nick lay back into the grass, and folded his arms behind his head, squinting up at the sky. "It was Uncle Aaron. He found her in the morning. He called 911, but she'd already been dead for hours."

I closed my eyes, feeling myself in Haylee's bedroom. I could see Aaron opening the door to wake Haylee up for school, and then there she was, lying on the bed, all still and cold. I'd been looking to Bradley for answers, when Nick knew more than either of us.

"I should have called her that day," Nick said. "I keep thinking, if she'd known how much we loved her, if she'd known she wasn't alone . . . Why didn't I call?"

"You didn't know," I said. It felt strange, me trying to comfort Nick when I felt exactly the same way. I should have—

"I should have known," he said. His voice lowered. "She told me she wanted to die."

I sat perfectly still. The wind blew a leaf across the grave in front of us.

He *knew*? "What?" I asked. "When?"

Nick shook his head, realizing my meaning. "No! I mean, not that day. Like a month before. She said she didn't mean it, but I shouldn't have believed her."

I ripped on a patch of grass so hard the roots came up. The tip of an earthworm sucked deeper into the sod, away from the light. "She used those words?" I asked. "She wanted to die?"

"Yeah," Nick said. "I should have told someone. But you know how Haylee exaggerated things."

A part of me thought, *why didn't you tell?* If he had, she might still be alive.

I let go of my handful of grass. That wasn't fair. Haylee had said similar things to me, if not in those words. "She was always talking about how I'd miss her when she made her exit. I thought she was just being dramatic, but I should have known what she meant."

Nick pulled a hand from behind his head and reached it toward me, like he was going to take my hand, but instead he just let it lie in the grass. He looked down at it, like it had betrayed him.

I took the opportunity to watch him while he wasn't watching me back. His eyes were dark, not like Bradley's clear blue. But a ray of light passed over his face, revealing different colored spots of brown and blue.

I wondered what would happen if I reached out and brushed his fingers. Would he grab on? Would he pull me into him?

Would holding on to each other keep us both sane?

The tips of my fingers twitched. But I couldn't be sure what he wanted. He was a boy; he was older than me. If he wanted to make a move, he could.

I stayed still; he stayed still. Whatever crackled between us soaked away into the silence of the graveyard.

"Don't blame yourself," he said finally.

"How can you say that right after you got done telling me how it's all your fault?"

Nick smiled. "Shut up. Just let me feel bad, okay?"

"You couldn't have known."

"But who else do I blame?"

I lay back, resting my head on the grass. "If you figure it out, let me know."

Nick rolled over onto his stomach, kicking his long legs out so his toes dug into the new sod. He propped himself up on his elbows, picking his wilted blade of grass apart with his nails, a millimeter at a time.

He was so close, now. Only a few inches away. I rested my arm in the grass between us, a hair's width away from his sleeve. It would be so easy for him to shift in my direction, and then we'd touch. We'd be connected—the only two living souls in the cemetery.

Nick got to the end of his blade of grass, and he blew the last piece in my direction. "I don't really know what to do now," he said.

And I nodded. "That makes two of us."

Eight Months Before

On a Wednesday in April, Mom was waiting for me in the living room when I got home, a magazine spread across her knees.

"Hey," she said. "Practice went late today."

"It got out early, actually," I said. "So I went over to Haylee's."

Mom paused for a moment. "Haylee can come over here, you know. You don't always have to hang out at her house."

I dropped my backpack on the floor next to the couch. "I know," I said. "It's just easier to walk over there after practice."

Mom raised an eyebrow. "And on weekends. And over breaks. And during the summer."

"You're mad that I went to Haylee's too much *last summer*?"

"No," Mom said. "I'm not mad. I just want to make sure you know she's welcome over here. I think I've only seen her once in the last month."

"And that was last weekend," I said. "Not that long ago." Haylee had walked over to give me a math assignment after I'd stayed home from school to ice my pitching arm.

Mom closed her magazine. "I'm worried about her. She had some scratches on her wrist."

That's what this was about. Mom wanted Haylee to come over so she could play psychologist. "I know," I said.

Mom folded her arms. "Do you know how she got them?"

"She cut herself," I said. "Her parents know. It's not a secret."

Mom studied me, as if trying to decide if I was lying. "And do you ever think about doing that?"

I shuddered. Split open my own skin? I didn't know how Haylee did it without passing out. "No," I said. "No way."

Mom nodded, satisfied. "I think I might call her mother, just to make sure she knows."

"Don't," I said. "That won't help."

"You don't know that," Mom said.

"Believe me. I do."

"Hazel might be glad to know that other adults are looking out for her daughter."

"If you think that," I said, "then you don't know her very well."

Mom narrowed her eyes at me. "What exactly don't I know?"

"She doesn't want anyone to know that Haylee has problems," I said. "She's got Haylee seeing therapists and doctors and taking medication, but it's all supposed to be this big secret. And she doesn't want you talking to Haylee because she knows you work with this stuff, and you'll figure out that their family isn't perfect." That was part of the reason we hung out there and not here. Otherwise, Hazel was always bothering Haylee about where we'd been and what she'd said, especially to Mom.

Mom sighed. "No family is perfect."

"You don't have to tell me. But leave Haylee alone."

"Okay," Mom said. "But if Haylee stops seeing a therapist, you let me know, okay? I want to make sure she's getting the help she needs."

"Fine," I said. And I ducked out of the room before she could pump me for more information about Haylee.

Mom *was* nosy. Maybe Hazel did have a point.

Chapter Nine

Mom and I have this Christmas tradition: on Christmas Eve we'll go to the home of a family—maybe someone who needs cheering up, or who doesn't have a whole lot of extended family around—and we take them sugar cookies and hot chocolate. Mom started the tradition fifteen years ago, which was both the year I was born, and the year she split up with my father. I obviously didn't make cookies that year, but Mom said she let me shake the bottle of sprinkles. Mom said we did it because traditions made families stronger, but I was pretty sure helping other people just made her feel better about herself.

Mom caught me in the kitchen on Christmas Eve morning, downing Pop-Tarts.

"You're having a nutritious morning," she said.

"It's Christmas," I said. "Should I be eating spinach to counter-act the cookies?"

"You should be eating protein," Mom said, "in preparation for this evening's sugar rush."

She had me there.

"You could make eggs," I said.

Mom nodded. "I think I will."

And as she was breaking the shells carefully over the pan, she let this drop: "I was thinking we could take cookies to Haylee's family tonight."

I took a long sip of my glass of milk. I should have realized that's where we'd be going.

Mom dropped the egg shells into the trash. "Is that all right with you?"

"Yeah," I said. "It's fine." I want to say I was thinking about how nice it would be for Hazel and Aaron to know we cared, or how I wanted to let them know I still felt like they were part of my family. But truly, all I could think about was the journal. If Hazel invited us in, this could be my chance.

Mom whisked the eggs with a wooden spoon while I broke the crust of my Pop-Tart into tiny, tiny pieces.

This time, I was bringing a purse.

Mom let the eggs cook and mixed up some orange juice, which I obviously couldn't drink with Pop-Tart mouth. Instead I grabbed the Christmas boxes out of the closet, and started sorting our fake-tree branches by length. I'd have preferred a real tree, but Mom was allergic. Mom seemed to think that plugging in a pine air freshener amounted to the same thing, but she used the same one every year, so by this time it barely smelled at all.

That's what I should have gotten her for Christmas. A refill.

Mom brought me a plate of eggs and helped me put the branches onto the tree trunk. She started wrapping the string of lights around and around while I opened up the boxes of ornaments. Mom gave me a new one every year, and she hadn't thrown away one single ornament that I'd made as a kid. They were all there, jumbled together in heaps: the construction paper wreath with the malformed marker-drawn berries, the paper-mache snowman with the dented head, even the single seashell sequin I had hung on a hook about four times its size.

That sequin had been a gift from Haylee, the largest sparkle from a pack of sequins she'd brought to school for an art project when we were seven, just months after we became friends.

The rest I could have thrown away, but that one would stay forever.

The ornaments amounted to four boxes of tangled hooks. They could have come from ten kids, instead of just one.

"I think we need to start a new tradition," I said. "Every year, we throw five ornaments away."

Mom's arms stretched far over her head as she wrapped the lights around the top of the tree, passing them from hand to hand. "Which would you suggest?"

From beneath a pile of paper snowflakes I extracted a wooden Santa on which I'd glued so much glitter that it shed as I pulled it from the box. The thing had been shedding every year since I was four, and still the glitter was thicker than the wood.

Mom laughed. "You spent two hours on that thing. All the other kids at your preschool drew a line of glue and wandered away. I had to pry you away from it when I came to pick you up. You just kept insisting that you weren't *done*."

"And you have a story like that for all of these?" I shook the cardboard edge of a box; hooks and bells jingled within. On the top I found the ornament Mom had bought me last year—a teddy bear wearing a catcher's mitt and holding a bat. There was no reason to wear a mitt and hold a bat at the same time, but apparently the people in the sweatshop where it had been made didn't know that.

Mom rested the lights on the floor, with only the top half of the tree wrapped, and came over to look in the boxes. She pulled out a paper chain made from construction paper so faded, I could no longer tell the red links from the green. "I don't have a story for this one," she said. "Except that you made about a million of these. All I had to do was give you a stapler, a stack of paper, and some scissors, and soon there'd be paper chains draped all over the house."

"Does that mean I can't throw it away?" I asked.

"Hey, I only kept one," Mom said. "Be proud of me for showing restraint."

If this was restraint, she was hopeless.

Mom poked through another of the boxes, and dug out a plastic Christmas tree. I'd scribbled all over it with markers, and glued rhinestones over every inch, in no particular pattern. "I have no story about this," she said.

I stared at it. "Haylee's ninth birthday party," I said. Her birthday was right before Thanksgiving. She'd made an ornament identical to it, which hung in her bedroom window for years. Her mother wouldn't let her hang it on the tree—she liked their tree to look perfect.

"Ah," Mom said. "So that stays."

I sighed. "Who are we kidding? We're just going to hang them all." And I started draping ornaments over the top part of the tree, where Mom had already hung the lights. Mom finished wrapping the bottom of the tree, and then ran up to her room and came down with a little white box: my new ornament for this year.

Mom hesitated before handing it to me. "I bought this months ago. I thought about getting you a different one, but I wasn't sure . . ."

I took the box from her and opened it. Inside, lying on top of silver tissue paper, was a pair of gold painted tragedy and comedy masks.

Mom bit a nail. "You and Haylee went to all those plays last summer, and you have every softball ornament on the planet—"

"It's perfect," I said.

Mom looked relieved.

I wasn't just saying that. Haylee liked theater, and I liked to go see theater with Haylee. The tragedy mask was the perfect symbol for the end of this year. Anything happier would have felt like a lie.

I hung it near the top, next to the tacky rhinestone Christmas tree. "Thanks," I said.

Mom gave me a surprised smile.

"What?" I asked. "I can't be grateful?"

"Of course you can," Mom said. And she busied herself untangling a chain made of misshapen clay beads that I didn't remember making.

We hung ornaments until all that was left in the bottom of the boxes were hooks and stray limbs of dismembered ornaments. The masks stared at me—the two halves of Haylee, one grinning, one crying. Mom plugged in the lights, which glowed beneath the thick layer of memorabilia. The one benefit of having a fake tree was that it looked the same year after year. Our Christmas tree, in all its tacky glory.

And I guess Mom was right about traditions holding people together, because of all the moments in the year, this one made us feel most like a family. Mom sat down in the living room. "Do you think we should take anything special over to Hazel's?"

Hazel's. Not Haylee's. "No," I said. "I think the usual cookies will be fine."

In truth, the only thing I wanted to carry over there was a purse. I spent the afternoon in my room, searching for the perfect one.

The trick was to take one that was small enough not to attract attention, but big enough to fit the journal in without looking like it was leaving far fuller than it had come.

Eventually I settled on a khaki bag, with a strap long enough that I could wear it on the opposite shoulder. I put in my wallet and keys and the school copy of *Tess of the D'Urbervilles* that I should have returned before break. If I wasn't going to read it, it could at least form my bag into the right general shape.

There were several cars in the Ricks' driveway as we pulled up their street. As we traipsed up their walk we passed the front window, and I could see Haylee's grandpa sitting on their couch. He always creeped me out, maybe because he always said my name real loud like he knew me, even though I never said a word to him. Today, though, I was glad to see him. More people meant more distraction; it would be easier for me to sneak upstairs.

Mom raised her hand to the doorbell, and I could hear "Jingle Bells" ringing through the door.

"I'm sure they'll appreciate the thought," Mom said to herself. She must have been pretty nervous about it, because she pasted on a big fake smile. I was glad I was the one holding the cookies—you appear less useless when you arrive bearing sweets.

Hazel opened the door and looked at us in surprise. When she saw the cookies, she smiled and got all teary. "Oh, Patty," she said to Mom, "You didn't have to do that." And even though she had real tears in her eyes, her smile was as fake and plastic as Mom's. "Come in, come in," she added, and ushered us in before we had time to sigh in relief.

Usually Haylee's living room glowed at Christmas, every inch of space filled with matching decorations until it looked like the holiday section of a department store. This year Hazel hadn't put up any decorations besides a sparsely-dressed tree, strung with a couple strands of lights and some silver balls.

Hazel flitted around the back of the couches, making sure everyone was comfortable. She was that kind of hostess—always taking care of everyone else, but you knew she was only doing it because she was supposed to and not because she really cared.

Nick leaned forward on the couch, catching my eye from where he'd been hidden behind his grandpa. He wore a shirt with rows of tiny numbers on it. I wondered if I should go talk to him, but he was squished between his grandfather and the arm of the couch, so the only way to sit near him would be to perch on the couch arm with my butt against his arm, which would be way more flirtatious than I was capable of being in a room with this many people.

The other couches were occupied by Haylee's other aunts and uncles. I knew some of their names, and recognized the others. I didn't know any of them well enough to talk to them, and even if I did, I didn't know what to say. Merry Christmas? Sorry Haylee isn't here? The only way to be sure I wasn't saying anything stupid was to keep my mouth shut.

I didn't see Aaron—again.

"Kira!" Haylee's grandpa said, leaning toward me. "Come in, for crying out loud." Nick shot me an apologetic glance, and that's when I realized that I was still standing in the entryway, while Mom had stepped into the room.

Hazel stood close behind me—if I stepped back, I'd stomp on her feet.

"How are you doing?" she asked in my ear.

"Fine," I said. I'd have the magic worn out of that word by the New Year, for sure.

"Haylee's dad is out in the garage," Hazel said. "Maybe you could talk to him."

I looked at her over my shoulder, stunned. "Are you sure?" I asked. "If he's hiding in the garage, does he really want to see me?"

"At this point," she said, "I don't see how you could make things worse."

I slipped through the hall and into the kitchen. If Hazel wanted me to talk to Aaron alone, she obviously hadn't found the journal. Talking to him alone would give me the perfect excuse to sneak around afterward, and grab it from upstairs.

I walked through the kitchen and opened the door to the garage. Aaron sat on top of their chest freezer with his feet on some boxes, a cigarette in his mouth.

I'd never seen Aaron smoke before, and he was a pitcher in college—an athlete—so I'd have thought he'd be more health conscious. That explained the garage, though. Hazel would never let anyone smoke in her house.

Aaron looked up at me as I opened the door, blowing a puff of smoke in the opposite direction. I tried not to make a face at the smell. I really don't get how people can breathe that stuff into their lungs on purpose, since it doesn't even smell good. Incense, maybe. Cigarette smoke, definitely not.

I watched Aaron from the doorway, waiting for him to yell at me or say something—anything to tell me whether I should stay or leave.

Aaron gave me a sharp nod and looked down at his feet, smashing his half-burned cigarette into the ashtray next to him. The tray was full of cigarette butts, and I wondered exactly how long he'd been sitting here, just smoking. "Hi, Kira," he said.

"Hey." I searched for something else to say. I spent a lot of time with Aaron, but we didn't really *talk*, unless it was about my pitching form, or game strategy, or what I needed to drill next. None of that told me how to act, now. I wanted to make him feel like I understood what he was going through, but the truth was, I had no idea. I wasn't sitting and smoking in the garage.

Just when I was about to step back, shut the door, and pretend I'd never gone out there, Aaron motioned me forward. "Come on out," he said. "You're letting the smoke in the house."

I closed the door behind me and sat down on a little metal stepladder in front of a pile of boxes.

"How's pitching practice?"

"Okay, I guess," I said. "I haven't been practicing as much as I ought to."

Aaron nodded, then reached down and plucked his cigarette out of the ashtray, relighting it. "You need any help?"

I'd have said yes to just about anything that would get him out of this garage. "Yes," I said. "I can definitely use it."

Aaron took another drag, and blew the smoke up toward the rafters. "Come over some afternoon and we'll practice."

"Okay," I said. "You mean after you get off work?"

Aaron gave me a long look, then shook his head. "I'm taking some time off."

I wondered if he had already planned that for Christmas, or if they gave you days off work when your daughter died. "Okay," I said. "How about Friday?"

"That's fine." He lowered his hand, flicking ashes into the tray.

Neither of us had said anything about Haylee, which felt wrong. Still, I didn't know what I could share with him. The only helpful thing I'd heard anyone say so far was what Bradley said.

It was worth a try. "This really sucks," I said. Aaron raised his eyebrows. "About Haylee, I mean. And everyone is acting like we all just need to move on, and that sucks, too."

Aaron closed his eyes and took another long drag on his cigarette. It was then that I noticed the deep bags under his eyes, like his whole face was filled with fluid. His skin had a gray tone to it that might have been from lack of sleep, or maybe prolonged smoke exposure.

"Yeah," Aaron said. "I guess it does." Aaron waved his arm through the cloud of smoke that hung in the air around him, causing frantic little eddies to spiral away. "You should get back inside," he said. "I'll see you Friday."

I wanted to say something else, something that would make everything better and convince him to come in the house and smile and act like it was Christmas. But I knew I couldn't, so instead I just said "Thanks" and headed toward the door. As the door cracked open, streams of smoke shifted through the air around Aaron like little dark spirits.

"Merry Christmas," I said. Then I closed the door behind me.

Eighteen Months Before

The summer I turned fourteen, my mother couldn't afford for me to be on the community team any more, so Aaron offered to sponsor me. He paid my fees for the regular season, and for the tournament season as well. Mom was so grateful to him that she let me spend twice as much time practicing, to show him that I was using his investment wisely.

In June, Aaron and I were practicing in Haylee's front yard, getting ready for the first big tournament of the year. My arm was off that day, so Aaron kept reaching way out of the strike zone to catch my wild balls.

"Watch your landing leg," Aaron said. "Finish tall."

Pitching is all about physics—you have to use your body just right to move the ball with a mixture of velocity and control. I wound up again, concentrating this time on my posture at the moment I let go of the ball.

Haylee sat down on the front porch. She often sat there, watching us, but today she was glaring. She looked from Aaron to me, put her head in her hands, and sighed a sigh that Mom would have described as passive-aggressive.

I don't know if Aaron noticed the glaring, or just got sick of reaching to catch pitches that should have floated into his glove. Either way, he called a break, and went inside for some water.

I sat down next to Haylee on the front steps.

"Not going well?" she asked.

"Brilliant deduction," I said.

"I can't tell the difference in the pitches," she said. "Just on your face."

"Well, if I pitch like that at the tournament, I won't get left in for an inning."

"You guys are going to be gone *all* weekend?" Haylee asked. That's what the sighs were about. She already knew that we would—the tournament was up in Redwood City, so all the girls were staying in a hotel.

"Yeah," I said.

"Figures."

"Why don't you come?" I asked. But Haylee shook her head. She'd come to a tournament once last year, but she hadn't wanted to hang out with any of the other girls, only me. She ended up watching movies with her dad all night instead, and didn't speak to me for two weeks after.

She gave another laborious sigh. "Everyone knows what's going on, you know."

"What do you mean?" I asked. I braced for nastiness. When Haylee felt left out of things, she got mean. But nothing prepared me for what she was going to say.

"It's obvious to everyone the way he's coming on to you."

I wrinkled my eyebrows. "Who?"

She looked at me like I was the biggest idiot in the world. "My dad. Why do you think he pays for all this?"

I should have told her it was a sick thing to say. But I just sat there, my skin growing cold. It wasn't true, was it? Aaron might as well have been my dad, just like Haylee was practically my sister.

She sat there, waiting for my reaction.

"It's not like that," I said finally.

Haylee jumped to her feet. "Fine," she said. "Don't believe me. You'll see." She ran into the house and slammed the door.

I sat on her porch, shivering. When Aaron came back out, I shook my head.

"I'm not feeling so great," I said. "I'm going home."

He said something about hoping I'd be well enough for the tournament, but I was already on my way down the driveway.

The next time I saw Haylee, she was smiling again. She didn't mention the things she'd said, and I could almost believe that conversation had never happened.

But at the tournament, I made sure to stay with at least one of the other girls at all times, unless I was out on the field. It couldn't be true, what Haylee said.

But if it was, I sure didn't want to find out.

Chapter Ten

When I returned from the garage, Hazel was in the kitchen, washing her hands. She looked up at me hopefully. "How did it go?" she asked.

"All right, I guess," I said. "How long has he been like that?"

Hazel's eyes dropped to her hands. "He's having a hard time."

No kidding. "We're going to practice in a few days. At least that'll get him out."

Hazel smiled. "Good. That's exactly what he needs. A nice reminder of what normal looks like."

I wanted to tell her that things would never look normal again, but that couldn't be true. Of course we'd all find normal. A new one, without Haylee. A normal in which she might never have existed at all.

That reality was worse than the funeral.

"Well," Hazel said, stepping toward the door that led to the living room. "I'd better see if they need anything."

"I'm going to use the bathroom," I said, moving toward the door to the hall. Hazel disappeared toward her guests, and I slipped off to find the journal.

I listened at the door to the hall, and heard nothing but the chatter coming from the living room. I moved down the hall and up the stairs as quietly as I could.

When I reached the second floor landing I stopped again, listening. The lights upstairs were all out. That was a good sign. I left the lights off as I headed down the hallway, feeling my way along with my hand until I reached the first door on my left—Haylee's door.

The light flicked on over my head and I jumped about a mile. Nick stood at the top of the stairs, tilting his head at me.

"Hey," he said. "I wondered where you went."

I'd been in the garage long enough for everyone to miss me. I should have made a reappearance before slipping away. "Um, I needed to use the bathroom," I said.

"In the dark?" he asked.

Crap. It was *more* suspicious that I hadn't turned on a light, not less. "I guess I missed the switch."

My excuses sounded guilty, even to me. My eyes fell on the numbers running down his shirt in tight rows. There was a good distraction. "Hey, what's that?" I asked, pointing at it.

He smiled. "It's pi."

"Ah." Now that I looked closer, I could see the first few numbers were 3.14.

"Look closer," he said.

I spent an unhealthy amount of time staring at Nick's pecs. *Again.*

"Can you see it?" he asked.

"See what?"

"The symbol."

And then I saw it. Some of the numbers were slightly darker than others, forming the outline of the pi symbol in the block. "Nice. You're not one of those freaks who has it memorized to the thousandth digit, are you?"

Nick shook his head. "I only know twenty-eight. And that's just because I was really, really bored in algebra."

"Right," I said.

"So," Nick said. He glanced at Haylee's door. "Going to visit?"

"Yeah," I said, seizing on the excuse. "I didn't want to ask in

112

the room with all those people . . ."

"Cool," Nick said. "Can I join you?"

Alone in Haylee's room. Again. I nodded, and Nick reached for Haylee's door. The handle clicked beneath his hand. Locked.

I let out a breath from the bottom of my gut. If I had to live in a house with Haylee's ghost, I'd lock the door, too.

Nick looked down at me. "Oh, well," he said. "It might be empty. I know Hazel was packing her things."

My hands shook. She'd probably gone through the room, piece by piece. Had she noticed the ceiling hatch? "I wonder where the key is," I said.

Nick gave me a strange look. "You want to get in there that much?"

Whoops. "No," I said. "I mean, yes, but—"

Nick moved into the bathroom and opened the medicine cabinet. He came back with a bobby pin, which he bent open and jammed into the lock.

I stepped aside. "You're really going to pick it?"

"It's not hard." He jiggled it in and out a few times, and the lock dinged. "Voila."

"Very impressive. Do you break and enter a lot?"

"My brothers lock each other out of their room all the time." He turned the knob and the door swung open. Nick held out his arm, letting me go first.

I stepped in and switched on the light. It wasn't empty. Quite the opposite—every drawer was opened, the contents spread over the mattress, the rug, the desk, the floor. The contents of the closet had been spread into piles, but only the clothes had been stuffed haphazardly into boxes.

A door closed downstairs, and I jumped.

Nick put a hand on my shoulder, steadying me. I held my breath, my arm tingling under his touch.

I counted the seconds. Two. Three. Four. No footsteps came up the stairs. And Nick's hand remained on my shoulder, squeezing it gently.

When I turned toward him, he'd bent down so his face was mere inches from mine. "Kira," he said. "Tell me what's going on."

My mouth might as well have been filled with cotton. I stared up at him, into his dark eyes. The room seemed to tilt, and if it weren't for his hand steadying me, I would have tipped right into his arms.

I was hopeless. That's what was going on.

Nick ran his hand down my arm, sending chills across my body. He took my hands in his and pulled them apart, running his fingers over my thumbnail, where I'd been picking at the cuticle so hard that it bled.

He held onto my hands. "You're nervous about something," he said. "Just like you were the day of the funeral."

My mouth fell open, but no words came out. My hands tingled every place where Nick's skin touched mine. And out of my daze came this thought: if I rocked up onto my tiptoes, I could kiss him. I could pretend I'd lured him up here on purpose, so we could be alone.

My head spun. *Do it*, I told myself. *Just do it.*

But my feet were glued to the floor. We stood there, suspended in time, looking at each other. And my heart fluttered for a frantic moment as I thought that *he* might kiss *me*, but he didn't.

"Is this about the journal?" he asked.

Cold air washed over me. I stepped back, and Nick let go of my hands. The space between us might as well have been miles. Before I could help myself, I was picking at my thumb again. "Why do you ask?"

Nick looked down at my hands. "Because you get twitchy every time I mention it."

I put my hands behind my back, but my fingers gnawed at each other there, too.

"Seriously," Nick said. "You don't wear secrets well."

He was right about that. I would have flopped myself on the bed, but with the mess scattered over it I had to settle for perching on one corner. "Okay," I said. "So I'm looking for the journal."

"Why?" Nick asked.

"Because," I said. "I'm worried about what Haylee wrote in there."

Nick raised his eyebrows at me.

I drew a deep, slow breath, and my mind began to clear. "About me," I said. "But it's nothing."

"You're this nervous over nothing?"

"Not nothing," I said. "Best friend stuff."

Nick scuffed his toe against the carpet. "Okay," Nick said. "So you came up here to look?"

"Yeah," I said. I swallowed. I didn't have to trust him. I could look in a drawer, or under the carpet again, or someplace else where I knew it wouldn't be, and then declare I'd been wrong. But my skin still tingled where he'd touched my hands. He wanted me to trust him. I wanted not to be alone in this. "But I don't have to look, exactly. I already know where it is."

Nick stepped farther away, leaning against the wall. "Don't let me stop you."

I looked at him in surprise. "You'd let me take it?"

He shrugged. "Whatever you're hiding, it must be pretty important to you."

"It is," I said. "I'll give Hazel the journal, just as soon as I pull out the stuff about me."

Nick just stood there, watching me.

"Promise you won't read it?" I asked.

Nick looked up at the ceiling, like he was weighing his options. He couldn't find it without me; if he could, Hazel would have by now. But I wouldn't show him where it was if he was going to betray me.

Finally, he nodded.

"Promise," I said.

"Okay, okay, I promise. Where is it?"

"Clear the floor," I said, pointing to the bottom of the closet. "There."

Nick moved aside a pile of clothing, and I extracted the chair from underneath a stack of books and dragged it over.

I stepped up to the chair, glad that this time I wasn't wearing a skirt. I planted one foot on it, and Nick immediately offered me his hand to help me up.

I took it, and our fingers clasped together. I practically floated onto the chair. When I let go of his hand to reach the hatch, I swayed, and Nick stood behind me with his hands on my waist to steady me.

I closed my eyes. I could turn around and step off the chair and into his arms.

But instead I pushed the hatch aside. Tiny filaments drifted down, and I ducked so they wouldn't fall in my eyes. I felt around inside the hole, but my fingers met only insulation.

"Let me try," Nick said. He stepped up on the chair behind me, one arm still around my waist, his entire body pressing against my back. My head leaned back against his chest instinctively, and his arm tightened around my waist.

I could feel his heart beating as fast as mine. The invisible barrier that always kept us inches apart had shattered. I couldn't move; I couldn't breathe. Nick put a hand on the closet shelf to keep us both steady.

His keys jingled as he pulled them out of his pocket. A tiny Maglite hung on his keychain, and he shone it up into the hole.

I stood on the very tip toes of my sneakers, using the shelf as a hand hold as I peered into the crawlspace. I dug my fingers through the layers of insulation. There was nothing here—only a rectangular indent in the insulation where I'd shoved the journal in.

My stomach sank. The hatch had been an obvious place to leave it. But if Hazel had found it and read it, she'd never be so friendly to me, and certainly not about Aaron. "It's not here," I said.

"Are you sure?" Nick asked.

He stood on his tiptoes, craning his neck as high as he could.

I looked back at his face. If touching affected him the way it did me, he didn't show it.

He planted a foot at the edge of the chair to boost himself up a little higher, and lifted the edge of the insulation, looking under it. "You're right," he said. "There's nothing here." Nick switched off his light.

The chair seemed to sink underneath me, dropping farther and farther away.

"Whoa," Nick said, and he grabbed me by the shoulders, holding me on the chair. "Careful."

I shrugged him off. Touching was worse than not touching, if it didn't mean to him what it did to me.

Nick stepped backward off the chair, and offered me a hand again to help me down.

I stepped down without it.

A toilet flushed downstairs.

"We need to go," I said. "They'll be looking for me." If Hazel found us standing there, she'd know I lied about the journal. I was about to move the chair back, hiding the evidence, but Nick beat me to it.

I blinked. He was covering our tracks, like he cared about getting caught. He wouldn't do that if he intended to turn me over to Hazel.

I locked the door behind us as we moved into the hall. I heard footsteps from the bathroom downstairs and flipped off the hall light, so no one would suspect that we were upstairs.

In the dim light from the bathroom, Nick eyed me. "You have insulation in your hair," he said. "Do I?"

He ran his hands through his own hair, and left me to do the same. We stood close, but his arms didn't brush mine as he dusted off his arms and shoulders.

The invisible barrier was back.

"Are you sure the journal was there?" Nick asked.

"Yeah," I said. "I'm sure."

"Haylee might have moved it," Nick said. "Maybe she threw it out, so no one would read it."

I picked at my thumbnail again. It felt slick in the dark, and

I wondered how much it was bleeding. "Maybe," I said. "You aren't going to tell anyone?"

"Why would I?" he said.

I smiled, and his eyes flicked down to my chin. Or my lips. Oh, heavens, Nick Harbourne was looking at my lips.

And over the hammering of my heart in my ears, I heard Nick's mom's voice from the hall below. "Nick?" she called.

Nick sighed, and maybe I imagined it, but he sounded a bit long-suffering. "I'm here," he said.

And he moved down the stairs, like nothing was wrong.

I leaned against the wall until I heard them go back into the living room. The image of Nick's eyes, lingering on my mouth, ran through my mind on repeat.

He *had* been thinking about kissing me, hadn't he?

When my pulse slowed and my hands stopped shaking, I moved silently down the stairs and back to the kitchen.

Four Days Before

It took Haylee forever to tell her mom about the Winter Fling. As a result, we didn't go shopping for the dress until the day before.

Hazel let Haylee use her credit card, and my mom drove us to the mall on Thursday evening. As we sat in the back of the car, Haylee said to me, "I wish you were coming to the dance."

I kind of wished I'd been asked, too, but only by Nick, and that clearly wasn't happening. "It's no big deal," I said. "I'm sure you'll have fun."

"Why aren't you going?" Mom asked from the front seat.

"Because I'm not allowed to date yet," I said. "Duh."

"You don't need a date to go to a dance," Mom said. "You could go stag."

I was pretty sure that word hadn't ever been cool. "That's not how it works," I said. You didn't just show up to the Winter Fling without a date. That was a sure way to end up sitting by yourself all night.

"The school only sells tickets to couples?" I could hear the feminist rising in her voice.

"No," I said. "But I wouldn't have anyone to dance with. That's kind of the point."

"You can dance with other people who don't have dates."

I sighed. "I don't really want to go, anyway."

"Fine," Haylee said. "Abandon me."

I rolled my eyes. Pleasing the two of them was impossible. "You'll have fun. Really."

Mom dropped us off at the mall and we arranged a meeting place for a few hours later. Then Haylee and I set off on a rampage through every store in the mall, searching for the perfect dress.

We had the usual problem. Every dress that looked halfway decent was out of Haylee's price range, and everything in her price range was all wrong: too skanky, too frilly, too bright, or too boring. She couldn't go looking like a whore, but she couldn't go looking like a cupcake, either.

As she tried on dress after dress, Haylee was leaning toward whore. She put on a navy blue dress that was backless and had a slit up each leg, so the front of her skirt looked like a loincloth.

"No way," I said.

"Are you sure?" Haylee asked, spinning and looking at herself over her shoulder.

"I'm sure. That dress is made of regret." I didn't mention that the loincloth look would make Fiona's leg wrap maneuver a lot easier.

In the end, Haylee found a black dress covered in silver sparkles on clearance that looked classy while still showing off her shoulders.

"What do you think?" she asked, spinning around in it for me. "Is this it?"

I stared at her. "We're meeting my mom in 20 minutes," I said. "We've been through every store. The dance is tomorrow."

She squinted at herself. "I don't know. Who do you think I'd be in this dress?"

I smiled. "I think you'll still be Haylee."

"I mean, do you think Bradley will look at me?"

"Looking at you is pretty much required for dancing."

"*Kira.*"

"*Haylee*. You look great. Bradley's going to die."

Haylee grinned at me in the mirror, twirling again. "You really think so?"

Did I really think so? I couldn't even picture the two of them together. "You're gorgeous. How could he not?"

"Okay," she said. "You've convinced me."

We spent our last few minutes looking for a necklace. Haylee chose this funky chain with a big silver medallion on it, which somehow managed to straddle the line between costume jewelry and flashy accessory.

"What do you think?" Haylee asked.

My phone beeped with a text from Mom.

And these were among the last words I said to my best friend in this life: "Just buy it already. We're ten minutes late, and my mother is pissed."

Chapter Eleven

When my cell phone rang on the day after Christmas, I hoped it was Nick. I pulled it off my desk and nearly dropped it again.

Bradley, the ID said.

Bradley. He hadn't called me since the party. But there'd been Christmas, which he probably spent with his family.

Still, if he was into me, shouldn't he have called after we kissed? If I was into him, shouldn't I have cared?

I answered. "Hello?"

"Hey, Kira," Bradley said. "How was Christmas?"

"Fine," I said.

Oh, no. I was using the F word on him. Not a good sign.

And then I said, "I mean—" right as he started talking again, so he stopped mid-word.

"Go ahead," he said.

"No," I said. "You go."

And then we sat there in awkward silence.

And this is what I thought: I cannot believe that I wasted my first kiss on Bradley Johansen.

But then he said, "I was wondering if you wanted to get in some practice today."

And my stomach dropped, thinking he meant practice

kissing, because obviously I must need that from how bad I'd been at it. But no. He meant softball practice. Or baseball, in his case.

I didn't want to make things totally weird between us. I was going to have to see him at school. So I said, "Sure."

And that's how I came to be pacing back and forth in my room in my warm-ups and sneakers when Mom yelled up the stairs: "Kira! Bradley's here!"

He was only fourteen minutes late this time, but I'd probably walked a mile across my bedroom floor. At least I got my warm-up in before practice. Aaron would be so proud.

When I got downstairs, Bradley was saying something to my mom about football.

I rolled my eyes. Everyone loves football, but I just can't bring myself to understand or care. Maybe because it's not a girl's sport, and even if it was, I have no desire to be pounced upon by members of the opposing team. We have rules against that in softball, because we're civilized.

"So where are you two going?" Mom asked.

"The park," I said. "He's going to help me with my pitching practice." Mom couldn't argue with that. It was practically homework, and homework was definitely not dating.

"Are you driving?" Mom asked.

"Slowly," Bradley said. "And with seat belts."

I had to smile at that. I grabbed my softball glove from the end table and swept past Mom and out the door. "See you later," I said. I'd probably hear about that later, but she didn't stop me from leaving.

"You look great," Bradley said, leading me to the car.

In my warm ups? "Thanks," I said.

On the way to the park, I went the rounds in my head. He hadn't made a move, which maybe meant he didn't want to kiss me, which was good, because I didn't want to kiss him, but maybe meant that he didn't want to kiss me because I was so *bad* at it, which was not okay at all.

123

We reached the park without any of those words tumbling out of my mouth, but I did pick at the stitching on my glove, and had to sit on my hands in order to stop.

After Bradley turned off the engine, he grabbed my glove off my lap and tossed it into his backseat.

Um. "Didn't you want to practice?" I said.

He shook his head. "Nah."

And then he climbed out of the car. I scrambled to follow, rehearsing what I needed to say to him in my head. *Bradley, you're nice, but I just realized I never liked you. Bradley, you're cute, but kissing you was gross. Bradley, I thought I was into you, but then I remembered that was Haylee, not me.*

Oh, this was so screwed up.

Bradley led me along the narrow path that wound through the arboretum. Trees grew all around, reaching up toward the sky and exploding in an umbrella of leaves. The trees shielded most of the noise from the park, so all I could hear was wind rustling through leaves.

"What are we doing here?" I asked.

Bradley smiled at me.

Ah, I thought. *What else?* And I tried to remember if he'd actually said the word softball when he'd asked me if I wanted to practice in the park.

Bradley moved closer. Something happens when you realize you're about to be kissed; your brain drains out your ears and you lose all sense of reason. I tried to speak, but my mouth just fumbled around, searching for any words, even the horrible ones I'd rehearsed.

As it turned out, Bradley didn't care if I talked. He stepped even closer to me, putting his hands on my waist and fixing his eyes on my forehead. I felt short of breath for a moment, like I was stepping up to the pitcher's mound in the first inning of an important game, and then he dipped his lips onto mine. And I tried to compose the words in my head, the ones that would make him understand: *Bradley, I don't want this.*

But before I could say them, he stuck his tongue into my mouth and twisted it around.

I had a sudden urge to bite it, but instead I pulled back. Bradley's face followed after me, moving down to my neck, kissing along my jaw line. And my neck reflexively leaned back, which he took as an invitation to travel down to my collar bone.

I gasped, and Bradley's hand snaked down and cupped my butt.

"Whoa!" I said, and I jumped back.

He laughed, smiling at me. "Sorry!" he said. "Didn't mean to scare you."

My heart overclocked. *Don't be stupid, Kira*, I thought. *He doesn't have a clue what you're thinking.*

So I put up my hands in surrender and said, "I'm kind of wound up. Can we talk for a while?"

He looked around behind us. "What? There's nobody here to see us."

"Still," I said. "I'm not comfortable . . ."

"Ah," Bradley said. "Let's go farther in."

And he took my hand and pulled me over a little low wall on the side of the path.

I didn't want to go anywhere with him, but I also didn't want him telling everyone at school that I was a total spaz who made a scene over nothing. So I sat down with one leg on each side of the wall, like I thought that was his intention all along.

Bradley gave me an annoyed look, but he sat down next to me. My hands pressed against the cold, grainy concrete, and the wind carried the cough-syrup smell of the eucalyptus trees. He'd been so upfront with me before, about Haylee, about everything. Why not just ask if I wanted to get together and make out? If given a direct opportunity, I would have told him no.

But I'd let him kiss me at the party. I'd acted like I enjoyed it. And I hadn't said anything here to make him think that I felt differently.

"I don't know what's wrong with me," I said. And I meant for that to just be the beginning, but Bradley was already in motion.

"Nothing," Bradley said. "You're perfect." He flipped one of his legs over the wall to match mine, scooting forward so our knees touched. For a second I thought he actually wanted to talk, but then he reached out and slid his hands under my thighs, lifting up my legs. He scooted forward on the wall and slid his legs under mine so I ended up sitting on his lap with a leg on either side of him.

That was too much. I didn't care if he thought I was a loser or not—I just didn't want him mauling me anymore. I shoved him by the shoulders and scooted back off his lap. My butt hit the wall, hard.

"Hey," Bradley said. "I thought you liked me."

I shook my head. "You said you wanted to practice."

"If you wanted me to stop, you could have said so."

Hadn't I said so? I couldn't remember now. I squeezed the wall between my thighs, concrete cold against my pants.

Bradley got this sad look on his face and said, "Hey, it's okay," but then he grabbed me by the wrists to hold me in place.

I hadn't thought about self-defense since seventh grade, but as Bradley clamped onto my wrists, I remembered what to do. Twist toward the fingers, my gym teacher had said. That's the best way to break someone's grip, even if they're stronger than you.

I twisted both arms inward and broke free of Bradley's hands, then threw my weight toward the sidewalk. Since my legs were still on either side of the wall, I fell down palms-first, tearing my pants along the thigh. Dirt and gravel embedded themselves in my hands and my arms ached from the impact, but I got my legs under me again.

"What the hell, Kira?" Bradley climbed off the wall and stood there on the path, looking down at me. I expected him to apologize, and to ask if I was okay, but instead he lifted me by the shoulders, dragging me to my feet.

I shook him off and did the other thing I'd learned in self-defense: I walked away.

126

Bradley walked after me, right on my heels. "Kira," he said. "Talk to me."

I spun around to face him. "Right. Now you want to talk."

He waved his hands in the air. "What's wrong with you? *You're* the one who won't tell me what's going on. I thought we were just having fun. I'm sorry if I did something you didn't want."

He said he was sorry, but his posture was defensive.

I took deep breaths. Maybe I was overreacting. I'd been so off-kilter that I didn't know if I was justified in being freaked out or not. If I could play it cool now, I might not have ruined things completely.

"Sorry," I said. "I'm just messed up lately."

Bradley put his hand on my shoulder, rubbing it. "I get that," he said. "I'm messed up about it, too."

Only this time, that didn't sound sincere.

"I want to go home," I said, stepping back.

His face hardened. "You were fine before. What's wrong with you now?"

"I don't want to be here," I said. "Maybe I *never* wanted to be here."

Bradley's face tightened in anger. I recognized the look. Haylee had worn it sometimes, when rage welled up, and all she wanted to do was hurt someone.

"Come on," he said. "You think you're better than Haylee?"

I took another step away from him, and a smile flicked across his face.

"What's that supposed to mean?"

"Oh come on," Bradley said. "She was a total slut. The whole school knew it."

I balled my fists. Haylee was a lot of things, but she wasn't that. "Haylee could barely even talk to guys."

"Sure, when she was sober. Ever see her at a party?" He feigned surprise. "No, that's right. You were never there. What kind of friend were you?"

My vision swam. "That's not true," I said, but I sounded less sure, even to me. Haylee drank when I wasn't there, sure. But that didn't mean she was throwing herself at every guy who came along.

But she only went to parties when I was doing softball, or away at cross-country meets. I thought she did it because she was bored.

Had she kept me out of that part of her life on purpose?

Please. Of all people, I wasn't going to believe the word of Bradley Johansen. He'd pretended he'd been nice to her, to convince me he wasn't responsible for what happened to her. But now I could see through him. Now I could see what he was. "What did you do to her?"

"Are you kidding? She'd worshiped me for years. I didn't do anything she didn't want me to."

I lost control of myself then, because I stepped right up into his face. "Haylee is *dead* because of you." My voice was edging on hysterical now.

"Whoa," Bradley said, holding up both palms. "It's not my fault she was so screwed up."

"No," I said. "You just went after her because you knew that she was." I didn't know how true those words were until I tasted them. I saw the truth mirrored on Bradley's face as well. His mouth opened for a comeback, but he must not have had one.

Instead, he shoved me by the shoulders, and I stumbled back.

I looked around at the trees. No one could see us in here; that was the point. So unless someone happened along in the next few seconds, I was alone with a guy who could overpower me in a fight.

"Leave me alone," I said.

"Oh, I'll do more than that," Bradley said, balling his fists. "I'll make you wish you'd never met me."

That's when I turned and ran.

One Year Before

For Christmas last year, Hazel got Haylee tickets to see a production of *A Christmas Carol* in downtown San Jose.

"It's stupid," Haylee told me over the phone.

"You like theater," I said. "Your mom knows that."

"I like *tragedies*."

I flopped back on my bed with the phone resting against my pillow. "Scrooge is all mean and stuff. That's tragic."

"And then he learns important lessons about life. And *changes*. What's that about?"

"I think it's supposed to give us all hope in the spirit of Christmas. You know. That if he can change, so can we." That sounded like the sort of BS that got me passing grades in English.

"Exactly," Haylee said. "But in the real world, people don't change."

"Okay," I said. "But you're still going to the play with your parents, right?"

"Yeah," Haylee said. "You want to come, too?"

"You just told me it's stupid, and now you want me to join you?"

"Come share in my misery."

"Sure," I said. I didn't tell her this, but I actually like *A Christmas Carol*. Not because of the schmaltzy ending, but because of the ghosts. Everyone else seems to think the show is happy, but I think those ghosts are terrifying.

But when I showed up at Haylee's front door on the night of the play, I could hear Hazel shouting in the kitchen.

"I gave you those tickets so we could do something nice as a family," she said.

Haylee shouted back at her. "Dad doesn't even *like* theater. Why can't you take us?"

"Because," Hazel said. "You're going to do something with your father for once. End of discussion."

I wavered on the doorstep, wondering if I should just go home. Haylee hadn't said that they only had three tickets, and I didn't mean for Hazel not to be able to go.

But Haylee saw me through the kitchen window and stormed over to the door.

"My dad's taking us," she said. "Hang on while I get my coat."

"I don't have to go," I called after her.

"No, you do," Haylee said. "Because if I have to sit between the two of them all night, I'm going to be the one who is dead to begin with."

On the way to the theater, Haylee sat in the backseat with me, fuming. Aaron was silent. I was convinced Haylee was going to ignore the both of us for the entire night. When we got to the theater and found our seats, I took the middle one, just to get her farther away from him.

Haylee tapped me on the arm. "Move over," she said. "I want to sit next to my dad."

So I moved, and Haylee sat between us with her hands in her lap, glaring down at the stage.

That was the thing about being Haylee's best friend; I let go of lots of things I didn't understand.

Chapter Twelve

At first I just ran like hell along the path through the arboretum. I didn't hear anything behind me—just the sound of my own sneakers on the pavement, and the shrieks of some children playing on the other side of the trees. I cut through some planter beds and several yards of grass to get to the sidewalk, and ran away from the park in the general direction of home.

I kept listening for the sound of an engine or the crunch of tires behind me, but no cars came. I cut down some side streets and looked over my shoulder. If he'd followed, I was pretty sure I'd lost him.

I picked gravel out of my palms as I walked. They weren't bleeding heavily—just oozing a little. My leg was killing me, and when I looked down I realized that I'd not only ripped up my pants when I'd fallen off the wall, but I'd scraped my leg up, too. My favorite warm-ups were totally ruined.

I should have worn something older, like my bulky sweatpants with the hole in the knee. Bradley wasn't worth this. Bradley wasn't worth anything.

Is that what Haylee thought, after the dance? She'd wanted him for so long—but if he only asked her out because he thought she'd sleep with him, he'd probably done the exact same thing to her as he'd done to me.

What would Haylee have done? Frozen? Cried? Gone along with it to make him happy?

How would she have reacted if he asked *her* what was wrong with her?

I could picture it a hundred ways, but I didn't know which was the right one. And then the knowledge settled over me, like a heavy weight: he'd gone after Haylee because he thought she'd be easy. He must have chased me for the same reason. He thought I'd be easy, because I'd just lost her.

He'd already made good on his threat: I did wish I'd never met him.

I slowed, getting my bearings, and beginning to shiver now that the adrenaline was wearing off. I was in a residential neighborhood a few blocks from a grocery store where my mom sometimes shopped. I could walk home from here, but my legs ached already. I pulled out my phone. Mom would have hers on, in case I needed to call. But if I called her so soon after leaving, with my clothes torn and my hands bleeding, she'd have a complete cow right there in the car, horns and udders and all.

There was only one other person I knew who had access to a car.

I opened a text message to Nick. *What are you doing right now?* He probably wouldn't respond. He was probably busy. He probably—

Talking to you? he texted back.

And though I was still picking grit from my palms, I smiled, and called him.

"Hey," Nick said.

"Hey," I said back. "Um, I feel bad asking this, but do you think you can give me a ride? I'm stranded."

"Sure," Nick said. I thought I detected sadness in his voice, like he'd hoped I was calling for some other reason, but it was probably just wishful thinking. "Where are you?"

I stopped on a corner with a bus stop and a bench and gave him the cross streets.

"On my way," Nick said. "How'd you end up there?"

There had to be a way to spin this that wouldn't sound like I'd been interested in Bradley. "I was practicing pitching with this guy from school."

"And he left you there?"

"Not exactly," I said. But my voice cracked, and with it my resolve to keep everything to myself. I let the whole story pour out, from Bradley calling me that morning, to him shoving me and threatening me.

The static on Nick's end increased, and I heard the choke and hum of his ignition. He'd put me on speaker, so he wouldn't have to get off the phone. Instead, he listened in what I could only imagine was stunned silence, peppered with questions.

"He tried to *kiss* you?" he said. "Wait, he did *what* to your legs?"

"I know," I said.

"You should call the police," Nick said. "You should turn him in for assault."

"No," I said. "I'm not really hurt."

"That's not what makes it assault."

I shivered. "I don't want to talk to the police. No one will believe me. He'll deny the whole thing."

"Still. He shouldn't get away with it." His voice had a defensive edge to it. No doubt his older brother impulses were kicking into full gear. "I mean," he went on, "what made him think he could kiss you?"

Oh, no. We were stumbling right into the other story. If I lied, and Nick found out about the party later from someone else . . .

"He thought that because I kissed him before," I said quietly. "I mean, after Haylee, but before today."

Nick was silent, and I knew what he must be thinking of me, kissing a guy who turned out to be so hateful.

"I don't know what I was thinking," I said.

"You kissed him before," he repeated.

133

"That doesn't mean I deserved what happened."

"No!" Nick said. "No, it doesn't. I didn't think that."

"Then what *do* you think?" I asked.

"I think—" Nick said. "I think—"

"Well?"

"I think I'm only a couple blocks away. I'll be there in just a minute, okay? Don't move."

"Fine," I said. That stupid word. I was obviously anything but.

Nick pulled up to the corner a few minutes later, and leaned over to open the passenger door for me. As I climbed in, Nick eyed my hands, which were cold and shaking. And also bloody.

"I fell," I said. Then I clamped my legs together, so he wouldn't see the hole in my pants.

"Jeez." He rummaged around between the seats and came up with a pack of wet wipes.

"What are you? A boy scout?"

"Thank my mom for that one." His tone turned serious. "Are you okay?"

"Yeah," I said. "I mean, I think I am now."

"Are you sure I can't take you to the police station?"

"No." It'd be my word against Bradley's. No doubt he'd already cooked up a convincing story about what a psycho I was, just like the zingers he'd told me about what a great date he'd had with Haylee.

Nick looked down at my palms as I cleaned them. The abrasions weren't all that bad. The things Bradley had said were much worse.

Nick spoke slowly, like he was choosing his words very carefully. "I'm sorry he did that to you," he said. "No one should treat you that way, but especially not someone you like."

"I don't like him," I said.

Nick swallowed. "Well, yeah. But you did, didn't you?"

"No," I said. "Haylee did. I just got confused." I squeezed my eyes shut. That had to be the final nail in the coffin. Nick would never want anyone so messed up.

"I'm sorry," Nick said.

"You didn't do anything."

"I know. That's the problem." He sounded truly miserable, like he had when Haylee was struggling, and he didn't know how to help.

I was tired of slipping into her place.

"Forget about me," I said. "What about Haylee?"

"Tell me again what he said about her?"

I tried to remember his exact words. "He called her a slut."

Nick wilted. "You think he attacked her, too?"

"I don't know," I said. "There has to be some way to know. Because if he did, he should pay."

"For what he did to Haylee, not what he did to you?"

"Exactly," I said.

"Um," Nick said. "I think you're missing my point."

"I'm serious!" I said. "There has to be some way to trick him into admitting what he did to her."

"I don't know," Nick said. "I think the best thing to do would be for you to focus on what happened to you."

Maybe. But I could handle it, and obviously Haylee couldn't.

"Kira?" he asked. He sounded so tired.

"I'm sorry," I said. "I shouldn't have dumped all this on you. I'm as bad as Haylee."

"Don't *say* that," he said.

"I didn't mean it like—"

"I know," he said. "I know. But I still hate that I wasn't there to protect you."

The older brother routine. I dug my elbow into the arm rest. "Thanks," I said. Though I wasn't any more thankful than I was fine.

Look on the bright side, I told myself. If Nick insisted on thinking of me as a little sister, at least I hadn't lost anything by telling him the truth.

Three Months Before

It happened during cross-country season. I'd run over to see Haylee after practice, still in my sweats.

As I reached her house, Aaron pulled up in his car, just home from work. He stopped me in the yard—I hadn't talked to him since he came to my last cross-country meet, a couple of weeks before. The sun set as we stood on the porch, catching up. I don't remember exactly what we talked about.

What I do remember is Haylee, waiting at the top of the stairs when we walked in the front door, like she'd been hovering there, listening.

"Hey!" I said to Haylee. "You mind if I shower before we hang out?"

That wasn't an unusual request. I showered at Haylee's place a couple times a week, trying to make time for her after practice, and I had extra clothes stashed in a bag in Haylee's bathroom just for that purpose. But Haylee just shook her head at me, like I was being too unreasonable for words.

"I've got some bills to pay," Aaron said, heading toward his home office. "But I'll be at your meet on Saturday, okay?"

"Okay," I said. I noticed that he hadn't even said hello to Haylee. The look on her face told me she'd noticed, too.

"I'm going to take that shower, okay?" I said. "I'll be in your room in a minute."

Haylee didn't say anything to stop me. She didn't say anything at all.

When I got out of the shower, I changed into clean clothes and headed across the hall to Haylee's room. I found her sitting on her bed, writing in her journal.

"Hi," I said.

She didn't respond—just kept scribbling. I borrowed her brush and ran it through my wet hair. She flipped a page. I parted my hair into two braids and secured them with bands from her dresser. Still she scribbled.

Finally she snapped the journal closed and put it away under the carpet in her closet.

"What were you writing about?" I asked, though I already had an idea. Haylee's shrink said she was supposed to write things down when they bothered her, like if she wrote everything down, it wouldn't live in her head and drive her crazy.

"You and my dad," she said.

My stomach turned. "What?"

"Oh, don't give me that," Haylee said. "You keep encouraging him."

I put the brush down on her dresser. Haylee was watching me carefully, waiting for me to respond.

"That's not true," I said.

"No? Why do you think he's always hanging around you? Do you think he actually wants to help? Please. Men never do anything for free."

I took a step toward the door. I could insist that she was wrong, but it would only add fuel to the fire.

"I'll see you tomorrow," I said.

"Why? You just got here."

"Because you're not being fair."

"I just write what I see. Does that bother you?"

That was a trick question. If it bothered me, she'd insist I was admitting guilt. But it did bother me, and we both knew it, so

137

if I said no, she'd accuse me of lying. "It bothers me when you write things about me that aren't true," I said finally.

"It is true," she said. "I mean, why wouldn't he want you, right? You're so much better at everything than me."

I turned around and walked out. I didn't slam her bedroom door, and I didn't slam the front door, either. But when I hit the street, I ran home so fast I probably would have qualified for varsity track.

At least I wouldn't need Aaron to coach me in that.

Chapter Thirteen

I went over to Haylee's house to see Aaron on Friday, even though my glove was still in the back of Bradley's car. As I walked over, I wondered what I was going to find. Would he smoke his way through pitching practice? Would he have to set down his cigarette to return the ball?

It didn't matter if we didn't practice at all. I had to talk to Aaron about the journal. He and Hazel must have found it in the crawlspace. They must already know what it said. And at least Aaron would be able to tell the truth from the lies, if Hazel couldn't; he knew he'd never touched me.

But now I had a more important question: what did the journal say about Bradley?

I jogged up to the front door and rang the doorbell, which still chimed Jingle Bells even though Christmas was over. No one answered the door. I bounced up and down on my toes, looking for movement in the windows.

If Aaron read *those* parts of the journal, maybe he didn't want to be seen with me.

I was about to ring the doorbell again, when the lock clicked and the door cracked open. Aaron's face peeked out, and I got a whiff of smoke, but at least he'd shaved.

Aaron looked a little surprised to see me, so I quickly said,

"Hey, I came over to practice like you said. If you've changed your mind, that's okay, but I need to talk to you about something."

Aaron shook his head, as if to clear it. "No, it's fine. Let me grab my glove."

"I forgot mine," I said.

"I'll grab an extra."

Aaron met me in the side yard, which had the longest piece of grass on the Ricks' property. If I stood close to the street, and Aaron put his back to the backyard gate, we could be as far from each other as I'd be from the catcher on the softball field.

Aaron handed me a glove.

"Maybe we could talk first?" I asked.

"Talk while you warm up," he said.

That was Aaron. All business. I should have known talking to him wouldn't be easy. I tucked my hand into the glove and flexed it. Mine had molded to my hand over the years. This one slid around. It'd been broken in by a hand much larger than mine.

Aaron walked down by the fence and turned to face me, tossing me the ball overhand. I took a step back and the ball hit my glove with a firm smack. I lowered my glove and wound up for the pitch as Aaron sank down on one knee, glove up and ready.

A bird hopped across the side of the porch, where Haylee used to sit and watch us. Until I looked, I could almost pretend she was there, cheering me on. She never cared much about softball, but she cared about me enough to make up for it. I swung my arm back, then forward, and released the ball. Aaron had to stretch his arm to catch it—way outside.

"That's all right," Aaron said. "It's just a warm up." He stood and tossed me the ball again. I caught it, and set for the pitch again.

This time I didn't look for Haylee. She wasn't there, and for a moment I could pretend that she'd gone in to bring us bottles of water, or glasses of lemonade, or to answer the phone. Soon she'd be back, watching for her dad's approval so she could cheer me for throwing strikes.

But Nick was right. Forgetting and then remembering again was worse than not forgetting at all. I just wanted to do what I'd come for and get it over with. But Aaron stood so far away, and I wasn't going to shout about the journal, or about what Bradley might have done. So instead of talking, we settled into a rhythm. Set, pitch, catch, throw, catch, set. I kept my eyes on the ball, as it cycled around—underhand toward Aaron, into his glove, overhand toward me, into my glove. His throws to me arced high over our heads, and my pitches to him—the good ones—floated straight to his glove, as if zipping along a flat surface.

With every pitch, it seemed like the grayness of Aaron's face got a little pinker. Would that fade when I told him what might have happened to his daughter?

My next pitch flew so wild that it soared past Aaron's outstretched glove.

"Focus," he said. "You had it there for a little while. Find the rhythm. To my glove."

To his glove. Just us and the ball.

I wasn't sure how long we practiced. I should have stopped, put down my glove, and insisted he talk to me. But the rhythm felt so familiar, I didn't want it to stop.

Finally, Aaron stood up from a catch, put a hand on his back, and said, "That's enough for today. Don't want to wear your arm out when you're just getting back into it."

"Okay," I said. "Thanks."

"No problem." Before, he would have added *anytime*. But maybe that wasn't the case anymore.

He turned and walked toward the house, and I drew a sharp breath. "Hey, Aaron?" I said.

He turned around. "Yeah?"

"Remember I needed to talk to you about something?"

He gave me a long look, and for a second I thought he was

going to say no, but then he motioned for me to sit next to him on the porch steps. I sat, waiting for Haylee's ghost to lean over my shoulder, but I didn't feel her.

"What did you want to talk about?" Aaron asked. He set his glove on his knee and looked down at the sidewalk.

"Haylee's journal," I said. "Did you read it?"

"No," Aaron said. "We never found it."

I tried not to look as surprised as I was. How could that be? They *must* have found it. Nick and I had dug through the insulation—even seen the outline of the place where I'd shoved it. But I couldn't say that without admitting that I was the one who hid it there in the first place.

"Oh," I said. "Because I was hoping Haylee wrote down what happened with her and Bradley Johansen."

Aaron's eyes narrowed. "What about it?"

"I think . . ." I said, "I think he may have, I mean, I don't know for sure, but—"

Aaron drew a sharp breath. "He had sex with her."

I was glad I was sitting, or I would have fallen over. He had *sex* with her? Haylee had sex, and she didn't tell me about it? "How do you know?" I asked.

"He admitted it to the police when they questioned him," Aaron said.

This time, my mouth dropped open. Why did no one tell me anything? "And they didn't do anything about it?"

Aaron reached into his pocket, pulling out a cigarette. He ran his hands over his other pockets, too, but didn't come up with a lighter. "What were they going to do? Teenage sex isn't a crime."

Maybe not, but if he pushed himself on her, that was. Haylee might have agreed to it; she was pretty much in love with the creep. But if Bradley mauled her like he did me, there was no telling how she'd reacted.

Unless she wrote it down.

"There's more," I said. "I hung out with Bradley a couple times in the last few weeks."

142

Aaron stared at his hands, twirling the cigarette between his fingers. "Did he say something to you about her?"

Ugh. How did I describe this? The story had spilled out too easily yesterday, but today I couldn't find the words. "He tried to make me do things I didn't want to."

Aaron's head snapped toward me, and I could see his jaw setting.

What happened to me *was* evidence of what happened to her, or at least, what Bradley was capable of.

"What exactly happened?" Aaron asked.

"Well, we kissed and stuff. I know that was messed up. I don't know why I let him do that. Anyway, we kissed a little, and then he wanted to kiss me more . . . I don't know. In ways I didn't want to, I guess." I hugged my knees to my chest.

"All he did was kiss you?" Aaron asked.

I froze up inside. Why was he asking? Was he jealous? I couldn't ever tell what was normal, coming from Aaron. The things Haylee said had warped my perception of everything.

"Yeah," I said. "When you say it like that it doesn't sound like such a big deal."

"No," Aaron said. "It is a big deal. You should stay away from him if he doesn't respect you."

When he said that, his voice rose a little, and I thought he might cry after all, but when I looked up at him his eyes were dry.

"I'm not going to see him anymore," I said.

He nodded sharply. "Good."

"But what about Haylee? There's really nothing the police can do?"

Aaron's face tightened. "You let us take care of it, okay?"

I shook my head. "But if Bradley did do something to Haylee, he shouldn't get away with it."

"He shouldn't," Aaron said, and he rubbed his temples so hard I thought he might wear off the skin.

I picked at the edge of the concrete step with my fingernail.

"Hazel has to have found the journal by now," I said. "She was looking for it. And Haylee never hid it that well—"

"Do you know where it is?" Aaron asked.

"No," I said. And for the first time, that was the truth. "But it had to be in Haylee's room, which means Hazel should have found it, right?"

Aaron squeezed the butt of the cigarette between his fingers. "If she found it," he said, "she didn't tell me about it."

I stared at him. Would Hazel herself hide it? Because if it wasn't me, or Nick, or Aaron, she was the only one left with access to that room, at least that I knew of. But why would she do that? She wouldn't be trying to hide the contents.

Unless there were also untrue things written in there about her.

"You could ask her about it," I said.

"Maybe when she gets back," he said. "She went to stay with friends for a few days."

She got away from Haylee's ghost. I looked at Aaron. A deep purple haze hung under his eyes. He should get away, too. Somewhere Haylee wouldn't follow him.

If such a place existed.

I sighed. "Could you call her? I just think we should gather some evidence against Bradley. I mean, if he raped her—"

Aaron jolted to his feet. "Let us handle it," he said. I opened my mouth to ask him what was wrong, but he stepped into the house and closed the door on me. Hard.

I sat there, staring at the door, feeling like I'd been slapped.

I looked up at Haylee's window, partially obscured by the tree, her blinds pulled closed.

And I began to formulate a plan.

One Year Before

On New Year's Day, I lay sprawled on Haylee's bed.

"Nick texted me last night," I told Haylee, turning my phone so she could see.

"Happy New Year," she read. "Yeah, he sent that one to all the cousins."

Oh. Of course. He hadn't been thinking specifically of me. "I guess it's nice to be included," I said.

"Well, yeah," Haylee said. "You're obviously part of the family."

And when Haylee wasn't looking, I deleted the text from my phone.

Chapter Fourteen

I could feel Mom watching me as I moved around the house on New Year's Eve. She paced behind the couch as I watched a movie. She hovered whenever I left my room for a snack. Christmas was the holiday I spent at home; I always spent New Year's with Haylee.

Mom might as well have said it. She was waiting for me to show signs of struggling—to reveal the inevitable cracks in the dam, and then she was planning to pounce in, wedge the crack open, and let it all pour out.

I didn't think it was that simple. I couldn't let go—wouldn't ever be able to—until I had Haylee's journal.

Obviously she hadn't told me everything. I could see that now, as much as it stung. Was Bradley the first guy she slept with? Or was he right about what happened when Haylee went out partying?

I had to have answers, and there was only one place left to look. I needed to hold in my hands the evidence of what happened to her.

Around eight, I sent Nick a text message: *What are you doing tonight?*

He replied: *Babysitting the siblings. Sorry.*

If Haylee had been here, I might have been invited. *I need to talk to you,* I wrote.

I'll see you at school. We can talk then.

I closed my eyes. He'd been so eager to talk to me when I'd texted him after the park. Was he jealous of Bradley?

No. He probably just thought I was a moron. I took the hint and only sent him one more message, at midnight.

Happy New Year! I wrote.

But he didn't text me back.

On the first day back at school, everything felt out of sync. Classes were the same. My locker was still in the same place, and the kids in my classes hadn't changed—except for the new haircuts, new clothes, and the occasional hair-bleaching. Even so, everything felt surreal, like a part of a past life. I floated to class in a state of déjà vu.

Several people stared at me and whispered as I walked by them to class. At least the gossip about Haylee hadn't died down. The only thing worse than the whispers would be if everyone forgot about her with the rest of the old news.

I didn't hear much of Mr. Craig's lecture. When he gave us class time to start the homework, I opened my book and stared at the problems. I pulled a piece of paper out and wrote my name on it. At least that much I knew.

Spencer climbed over Haylee's empty seat and sat in it, though I hadn't heard Mr. Craig announce group work. When I didn't look up at him, he tapped me on the arm. When I didn't respond he hissed in my ear. "Psst! Kira!"

"I don't know the answers," I said. "Sorry." Then I wrote the date under my name. That was two pieces of information down. Go me.

Spencer leaned over, setting an elbow on my desk. "Hey, it's a new year, you know?"

I'd dated my paper for January of last year. So much for that.

"There," I said, erasing the year. "Happy?"

Spencer shrugged. "Thought you might want to know."

I turned back to the book, copying down the first problem.

"So," Spencer said.

Already I wanted to sock him. He'd no doubt come to harass me with more horrible theories. He'd had all of Christmas break to cook them up. Maybe I should just grab the bathroom pass now and save us both the trouble.

Then Spencer continued: "Is it true about Bradley?"

My pencil froze on my paper, and my heart started to hammer. "What, that he's a loser?"

My eyes stayed on my paper, but I could see Spencer grinning at the edge of my vision. My cheeks burned.

"It *is* true," he said. "Man, I totally thought he was lying."

I finished making up numbers for the first problem and copied down the second, hoping Spencer would get bored and wander away to torment someone else.

He didn't. "Did you do it because of Haylee?"

This time I turned in my chair to face him, glaring at him. "What's that supposed to mean?"

He shrugged. "I just heard that sometimes people do crazy things after someone dies."

A couple rows away, someone was tittering. As I glanced over, Stephanie looked pointedly away.

"What did Bradley tell you?" I asked.

Spencer smirked. "Well, *Bradley* didn't exactly tell me anything."

Great. "Who then?"

"Stephanie."

Obviously. I wondered if Stephanie had heard the story from Bradley, or if the gossip had been traveling around for days. Luckily, they'd all been vacation days, which ought to have slowed the velocity a little.

"What exactly did you hear?" I asked.

For the first time, it was Spencer who looked down at his paper, not me. He stared at the first problem. He hadn't gotten around to copying it down yet. "That you two . . . you know . . . "

And from the way he said it, I did.

No, I thought. *No, no.* Would random juniors slut-cough at me in the halls, now?

A series of foul names ran through my mind. I'd hurt Bradley's pride, and now he was going to hurt mine. *That's* what he meant when he said I'd wish I'd never met him.

Spencer was watching me, waiting for a reaction, though I was sure it was written all over my face.

"It's not true," I said, but my voice sounded strange. My whole body went cold. My eyes started to burn. After all this time, I was going to start bawling in the middle of geometry. "It's not."

Spencer looked at me, and he must have seen the beginnings of the tears welling up in my eyes. He opened his mouth and muttered something unintelligible. If I hadn't been so upset, I might have reveled in the fact that for once in his life, Spencer was speechless.

"Spencer," Mr. Craig said. "Go back to your seat." Spencer's head snapped up to look at Mr. Craig. He looked caught.

As Spencer grabbed his book and papers and scrambled back to his seat, Mr. Craig squeezed between the front desks and sat down where Spencer had been.

"Are you okay?" Mr. Craig asked. "Do you need to go to the office?"

"He's a liar," I said. And then I realized that didn't answer either of Mr. Craig's questions.

"I'll talk to him," Mr. Craig said. It took me a moment to realize he thought I'd meant Spencer. "I'll give you a pass. If you don't want to come back, go to the counselor's office, okay?"

I nodded. The burning in my eyes receded. I dried the little pools from my eyes with the backs of my hands. My best friend had been dead for almost four weeks, and that was all I could muster—and over *Bradley*. Pathetic.

Mr. Craig patted me on the shoulder as he got up, and then walked over to his desk to write me a pass. No toilet seat this time, since I might not come back to return it.

I stuffed my book into my backpack and stood up, not looking at anyone, even though half the class was staring at me. This would probably be all over the school before the final bell rang: Kira slept with Bradley, and then she had a fit in class because he told everybody about it.

Mr. Craig handed me the pass and said, "Hang in there."

As I turned to go, Mr. Craig called Spencer over to his desk. Part of me wanted to turn around and watch, but I kept walking. Behind me, I heard Mr. Craig say, "Spencer, why are you such an idiot?"

And then Spencer said, "I come by it naturally."

No kidding. Must be self-awareness day.

I marched out of class, burning from my ears to my chin. How could Bradley say those things about me? If it wasn't true, why did I feel so dirty? I charged into the bathroom, hitting the swinging door with both my palms. And as I did, I heard a giggle fall to a hush.

Two hall passes sat on the metal shelf below the mirror—a yard stick and a stuffed penguin with the word "Wick" written across it in all capital letters. There was a whirring sound, like a quickly-pulled zipper. And two sets of breaths heaving—besides mine.

I bent down and looked under the stalls. In one, a pair of pointy-toed heels rested between a pair of wide, black Vans that looked exactly like Bradley's.

I stepped toward the door of the stall and gave it a swift kick, like I wanted to give to Bradley's groin. The door crashed into the couple, who let out a shout and a shriek. The girl turned away, so I only knew who it was by the frizzy volume of her hair.

Catherine.

Bradley bolted out of the stall, his eyes widening in shock when he saw me.

I stood in the bathroom with my arms crossed, glaring him down. "Hi," I said.

Bradley's neck was raw and red behind his left ear. Catherine's lipstick was smeared across half his face.

I hoped it was waterproof. Try to get *that* off.

Bradley glared at me, and I balled my fists to keep them from shaking.

Haylee was dead because of him.

It was Catherine who spoke first. "What do you want?" she asked. And I could tell from the venom in her voice that Bradley had already been feeding her lies. I wondered what story he could have told her that made it okay for him to maul her in a bathroom stall when he'd supposedly been having sex with me the week before.

Bradley stood practically on my toes. "What the hell are you doing?"

"Oh, sorry," I said. I let the full weight of my sarcasm drip from my voice, partly to cover my fear. "I thought I heard someone choking in there. Guess that was you."

"I thought I made it clear," Bradley said. "You don't own me."

"I don't want to rent you, either," I said. My voice was shaking, so I spoke faster, trying to cover it. I pointed at Catherine. "Neither should you. Or don't you think he'll spread the same lies about you?"

Catherine put a hand possessively on Bradley's arm, and Bradley's mouth twitched into the shadow of a smile.

I wanted to flatten Bradley's nose, then and there, but he was stronger than me. So instead I stared him in the eye. "I heard they found Haylee's journal."

The smile disappeared from Bradley's face. "Her what?" he said.

Watching him squirm gave me confidence. I kept going. "Her journal. Where she wrote down the details of everything that happened. You knew she was a writer, didn't you?"

Bradley's eye twitched.

I mustered a smile. "I can't wait to find out what Haylee wrote about *you*."

Bradley's lips parted, ever so slightly, as he understood my full meaning. And I was certain that was the closest to satisfaction I was going to get.

Now I managed a full smile. I couldn't help but be proud of that feat. "See you." And I turned my back on them.

"Hey," Bradley sputtered behind me. "Wait. What?"

But his words cut off when the door swung shut behind me.

I turned and walked down the corridor toward class, but stopped when I saw Fiona marching toward me, her pointy-toed boots clicking angrily on the tile.

I remembered now. Bradley and Fiona both had algebra with Mr. Wick this period. He must have been lax with his bathroom policy, because I'd seen them necking against the portable more than one morning on my way to class late.

As she approached me, Fiona gave a withering glare. I sighed, and did the only thing I could think of to do. I pointed toward the girl's bathroom.

"He's in there," I said.

Fiona's boots clicked louder as she marched past me, giving no further acknowledgment to my presence.

But I heard the bathroom door open behind me, and I ran back in the direction of geometry.

As much as I wanted to watch the fireworks, I didn't want to get burned, and I didn't want to be in the office when the lot of them got hauled in after the show.

Sixteen Months Before

t was about a hundred degrees outside the day Haylee and I walked to 7-11 in our flip-flops. Her mother warned us that she was about to leave the house for a few hours, but when we walked up to the front door, Haylee groped her own pockets.

"Nuh uh," she said.

I swallowed a mouthful of cherry Slurpee. "You didn't."

"I did. I forgot my key."

We walked around to the back door, and found it also locked.

"Call your mom?" I said.

"No way," Haylee said. "She'll be pissed. She told me to take it, but I still forgot."

The heat from the wooden deck soaked through my flip-flops and toasted my feet. "It's a million degrees out here. We'll melt before she comes back. Does a neighbor have the key?"

"Nick's mom has one." She gave me a sideways look. "You didn't steal my key just to see him, did you?"

I held up my palms. "I didn't even know they had a spare. I swear it."

Haylee smiled. When she called Nick instead of her aunt, I knew that was at least partly for me.

We were slurping the bottoms of our cups by the time Nick arrived. He unlocked the door, and then brushed my lips with his fingertip as he let us inside.

"Nice dye job," he said.

I pressed my own fingers where his had been, and checked myself in Haylee's kitchen mirror. My lips were stained bright pink from the Slurpee, but no more so than Haylee's.

And he hadn't said a thing about hers.

Chapter Fifteen

All morning I dug at my cuticles, waiting for an office aide to come and pull me out of class. But the note never came, and it wasn't until lunch that I heard Stephanie announce to a crowd that Fiona and Bradley had been sent home for fighting.

"She clawed him right in the eye?" Stephanie said. "You should have been there to see it?"

I should have been there. But if they were home and I was still here, the sacrifice had been worth it.

At lunch I avoided the quad and the cafeteria, in hopes of also dodging Catherine.

I found Nick sitting by himself on a planter by the portable classrooms. He had on a Superman shirt, but the "S" was backward. The cafeteria and quad were at the other end of campus, so while this area wasn't actually off-limits, the only group who bothered to eat here was a circle of guys kicking a hacky-sack.

As I walked up to Nick, he pulled an apple out of his backpack. That's when I realized I'd forgotten to pack lunch.

"Hey," I said as I walked up. "Your shirt's on inside out."

Nick smiled. "It's supposed to be that way. It's a Bizarro Superman shirt."

Sure enough, the seams weren't showing. I wasn't sure what

was Bizarro about it, but I didn't ask. "Can I talk to you?"

Nick moved over, even though there was plenty of room for me to sit. "Did you bring lunch?"

"I forgot."

"You can have half my sandwich. If Haylee were here, she'd have eaten it anyway."

I sat down, and he handed me a diagonal half of his peanut butter and jelly.

"Thanks," I said.

"No problem." There was an edge to his voice.

I hesitated. "I told you the truth about what happened with Bradley, you know," I said. "There was nothing else to it."

He nodded, but he looked relieved, which meant he already knew about the rumor. "You heard?"

I nodded. "It must be all over school."

"I wanted to punch the guy who told me."

I felt like I'd been gut-punched, myself. "It's fine," I said, although it was obviously anything but. "But I need your help."

"Yeah?" He asked.

"Yeah. I need to get the journal."

Nick looked confused. "I thought they already found it."

"I don't know," I said. "Aaron said they still didn't know where it was, which means if Hazel did find it, she lied to him about it."

Nick's eyebrows rose. "Why would she do that?"

Maybe the things Haylee wrote about her were as bad as the ones that she wrote about me. "That's what I want to know," I said. "That's why I want to get into her office while she's out of town. To see if she stashed it in there."

Nick sighed. "What exactly did you have in mind?"

I took a deep breath. "We need to get Aaron out of the house. Then we can break in and search."

Nick eyed my torn fingernails. "Must be some secret you're trying to keep."

It was an invitation to tell him, but I didn't accept. "Does your mom still have their spare key?"

"Ah," Nick said, studying his sandwich. "That's why you need my help."

"That's part of it," I said. "But it's not like I want to go alone. Plus, I'll need a co-conspirator to help me distract Aaron."

"No need," Nick said. "I heard my parents talking last night. Aaron's been going out drinking at night since Hazel left town. They're worried about him."

I cringed. "So I'm stealing from a drunk, now. That's lots better."

Nick looked me in the eye for the first time since I'd joined him. "I'll make you a deal," he said. "I'll help you get the journal if you tell me what's in it."

I was asking too much. I had to meet him halfway. "I'll let you read it," I said. "After we get it out of the house."

"And you'll talk to me about it. You promise?"

Deep breaths, Kira. Deep breaths. "I promise. We'll go tonight after it's dark?"

"Late," Nick said. "To make sure he's gone. I can meet you at eleven."

"Okay," I said. "Where?"

"I'll pick you up at your house. I'll tell Mom I'm sleeping over at a friend's so we can work on a school project."

I smiled. Cover for the whole night, plus a responsible excuse. "Better meet me on the corner instead of out front," I said. "I'm going to have to sneak out."

I looked down at our uneaten sandwiches, his half, and mine, waiting for Nick to argue. But he didn't. He just finished his apple, bite by bite.

Two and a Half Years Before

The summer I turned thirteen, Haylee and I spent the three weeks after tournament season ended at the rec center pool. Nick lived only a few blocks away, so he walked down and joined us in the afternoons, sometimes with his younger siblings, sometimes without.

Haylee and I were lying out on our towels, her in her pink sports-bra bikini top and swim shorts, and me in my one piece. I watched the entrance, waiting for Nick.

Haylee followed my eye line, and snorted. "He's not coming today," she said. "His grandma is in town."

"Oh," I said. "You could have told me."

"I just *did*."

"I meant *before* I got my hopes up."

She laughed. "It's not my fault you paddle around after him like a puppy."

My cheeks turned red. I did *not*. If anything, I avoided him too much, so he had no idea that I liked him. Though he did like to splash me until the lifeguards yelled at us to stop.

"Besides," Haylee said. "He's more likely to go for her." Haylee pointed up at a lifeguard, who must have been at least sixteen, wearing a swimsuit that pushed up her breasts.

"Really?" I asked.

"I know, right? But Nick likes older girls. He told me."

"He said that to you?"

Haylee's face fell, like she'd just now realized that would bother me. "Yeah," she said.

I lay my cheek down on my towel, with my face turned away from Haylee, so she wouldn't see my cheeks turning red.

"I'm sorry," Haylee said after a second. "It's not your fault you're younger than him."

After that, I stopped meeting them at the pool.

Chapter Sixteen

That night I stayed upstairs until I knew Mom had gone to bed, and then I cleaned the living room. Something about sneaking out in the middle of the night made me want to do something nice without being asked, but I didn't want to do it while she was awake, because then she'd give me that look that meant she knew I was up to something, and as always, she'd be right.

When Nick texted me, I was changing into black jeans and a hoodie. *On my way now,* he said.

When I reached the corner, a car approached down the street, headlights shining toward me. In the glare, I couldn't tell who it was. If it was a cop, I could be picked up for breaking curfew. I stepped back into the shadows of some bushes, but the bushes were shorter than I was.

The car stopped a few feet away. The passenger door opened, and I could see Nick inside, leaning across the seat to look at me, wearing black jeans and a black hoodie.

How cute. We were twins.

"You coming?" he asked.

I climbed into the passenger seat. "We look like criminals." All we needed were a pair of ski masks.

"But check this out." Nick unzipped his hoodie. His shirt

underneath was black, but on his chest was a picture of a phone booth and the letters "WWTDD."

"I actually get that one," I said. "Doctor Who." Haylee and I used to marathon it on weekends.

"I thought you would," Nick said. "Finally."

"I bet the Doctor wouldn't have worn all black."

Nick smiled. "I knew I should have gone with the bow tie, but I didn't want to be conspicuous."

As we cruised by Haylee's house, we both turned to look at the empty driveway.

"I guess that's a go, then?" he asked.

My heart picked up pace. "Yeah," I said. "Let's do it."

Nick drove around the block and parked at the far end of Haylee's street. "The neighbors will probably recognize the car," he said. "We should walk from here."

In our burglar clothes. This was going to be good.

Most of the lights were out on Haylee's street, but a few windows showed a television flicker. As we approached Haylee's house, I was relieved to see that all the lights were out. I felt exposed walking up the empty side yard. Nick led me through the gate, so we could go in the back door. The gate clicked shut behind us.

Nick paused on the other side of the gate. "What's that noise?" he asked.

I stopped, listening. A humming noise came from the house.

"Maybe they left a box fan running," I said.

"A fan. In January."

"A space heater?"

"If it is, it's the loudest one on the planet."

I followed Nick to the back deck. When we came to the steps, he pulled keys out of his pocket.

"Don't turn on any lights," Nick said, "in case Aaron comes home while we're here." Then he held the door open, and let me go in first.

I stepped into the kitchen far enough that Nick could come

in, too, and he shut the door behind him and punched the lock. We both breathed in at the same moment.

The house smelled of smoke. "Aaron must have been chain smoking in the house," I whispered. "Hazel's going to have a fit." Also, he had to be smoking the nastiest cigarettes known to man.

Nick nodded and looked toward the inside garage door. I could still hear the humming sound. Aaron was probably trying to use the fan to get rid of the smell. That wouldn't work. If it smelled this bad, it must have already sunk into the upholstery.

I put a hand on Nick's elbow, pulling gently. "Let's get this done," I said.

We moved toward Hazel's office. I kept my hand on Nick's elbow as we moved through the kitchen to the hallway, and past the empty downstairs bathroom. Had the house been dark and quiet like this when Haylee swallowed all those pills?

The hairs on my arms rose, as if she was beside me in the dark.

We reached the door to Hazel's office. I put my hand on the door frame, groping in the dark for the handle, but my hand met air.

The door was open. My fingers reached the lamp inside her door. I switched it on.

Hazel's office was a disaster. Papers were strewn over every surface—not just the desk, but the chair, the floor, the filing cabinet. Several of the drawers had been removed and stacked, their contents scattered across every available surface.

I'd never seen this office with so much as one paper out of place. "What happened?" I asked.

Nick stepped up to the desk and shifted the papers around. There were statements from the mortuary with numbers so high they made my eyes cross, as well as a mountain of cards and pictures and flowers. He unearthed an empty pill bottle and held it up. Xanax. Haylee had taken that one for anxiety once, but this prescription was made out to Hazel, and the date was recent.

I joined Nick, sifting through the papers on the floor,

searching for the journal. But my hands came up empty.

I closed my eyes, thinking about the enormity of the house, the number of places that Hazel could have hidden it.

"Look at this," Nick said. He pulled some papers out of one of the drawers. The drawer front was chipped at the top, and on closer inspection, I found the broken piece still attached to the front of the desk, secured by a locking mechanism. Someone had pried the locked drawer open with so much force that the press board split in two.

I looked at the papers in Nick's hands. A title ran across the top in bold letters: *Settlement of Divorce.*

My stomach dropped. Hazel was filing for divorce?

Now?

I looked around at the office. "Hazel didn't do this," I said. "It was Aaron."

"Oh," Nick said. "Oh, no."

He dropped the divorce papers onto the desk and brushed past me, running out of the office and down the hallway toward the kitchen.

Toward the garage, and that loud hum.

I followed, close on Nick's heels, breathing in the smoky smell of the house, which now that I thought of it, didn't exactly smell like Aaron's cigarettes. More like the school parking lot right after the final bell rang.

More like exhaust.

Nick got to the kitchen door that led into the garage. He opened it, the weather stripping dragging along the concrete step at the bottom. And over it, I could hear that loud humming.

Not a fan. A car motor.

Oh, no.

I coughed as my lungs took in air thick with exhaust. Nick flipped on the garage light, which framed him in the doorway, clouds of brown air rushing into the house around him.

There, in the garage, was Aaron's blue sedan. I stepped up right behind Nick, looking over his shoulder. Junk from the garage was piled on either side, wedging the car between boxes, bags, and tools. A stack of cardboard topped with a tarp was squished against the driver's side door, but all the car windows were down. And in the driver's seat lay Aaron, his seat back reclined, his head lolled over like he'd fallen asleep at the wheel.

His eyes were closed, and while Nick convulsed with coughs in front of me, Aaron didn't move.

My lungs hacked again, and I put a hand over my mouth. Nick breathed through the sleeve of his hoodie and climbed over the piles of junk toward the car. He reached in through the window, his face contorting and turning away from Aaron's body.

And he turned off the car.

Then he doubled over, coughing.

I stepped toward Nick, ready to grab him by the arm and haul him out before he fainted from the fumes. And that's when I saw it. There, on the dash, just a foot from Aaron.

Haylee's journal.

Nick reached over the pile of boxes next to the driver's side door again. His fingers stretched toward the body—toward *Aaron*. And when his hand met Aaron's neck, he flinched.

My stomach turned, and I coughed again. If we stayed here, we were both going to die. I reached for Nick, grabbing him by the arm. But before I pulled him back into the kitchen, I reached past him, dangerously close to Aaron's still body, and grabbed the journal.

Then I turned back toward the kitchen, hauling Nick along with me as we both sputtered and hacked. When we reached the kitchen door, Nick did what we should have done to begin with: he hit the button to the automatic garage door. The gears of the door opener ground as the door lifted, and the filthy air emptied out into the night.

I ran through the kitchen to the back door, with Nick right behind me. Nick closed the back door behind us, and we both breathed deep in the fresh air. My hand gripped the journal.

We'd been in the house with a dead body. No one would

believe we'd killed Aaron with the car, but if they read the journal, they'd think I was the reason he did it. They'd think I was
here, trying to cover the evidence.

Nothing I said would make them believe me, when Haylee
wrote those lies and wasn't here to deny them.

Nick already had his phone out and to his ear. I could hear
the operator on the other end: "911. What is your emergency?"

"My uncle killed himself," he said. "I found him in the garage
with the car running."

The operator said something, but I couldn't make it out.

"No," Nick said. "I opened the doors, but he's cold."

He's cold.

If he'd started with a full tank of gas, the engine could have
been running for hours.

My knuckles ached from my tight grasp on the journal. If
I let the police see me with it, they'd think it was evidence.
They'd think Aaron killed himself because of what Haylee wrote.
They'd think it was true.

I looked around frantically. What could I do with the journal?
I could hide it here in the yard, but anybody might find it. I
turned and walked toward the side yard. Nick followed, his ear
still to the phone. "Yes, I'll wait," he said.

I reached the gate, and pushed it open.

And then, with Nick standing too far behind me to stop me,
I ran.

Three Months Before

Haylee called my cell phone at two AM the Friday after the first week of school. I groped for it on my nightstand, only finding it on the third swat. "Hello?"

I could hear sniffling on the other end, but no words.

"Haylee?"

The sniffling grew softer.

"Haylee?" I said again.

Finally I heard her voice on the other end, though it sounded muted, as if far away. "Will it ever end?" she asked.

I didn't have to ask what. She meant the pain, the fear, whatever demons cornered her in the night and made her wake up screaming.

"Sure," I said. "You'll feel better tomorrow."

"No!" Haylee said. "Wrong answer! One strike, you're out."

"I get three strikes," I said, and I hoped she would laugh, but instead she sobbed like a wounded animal.

"I'm sorry," I said. "I can listen, if you want."

Her sobs fell silent. "You can listen," she said, "but can you hear?"

We sat there in silence. I watched my digital clock tick by one minute, then five, then fifteen. Haylee must have fallen asleep with her cheek against the phone, because I could hear her breathing grow deep and even.

So I never had to tell her that the answer was no. I could listen. I could try. But I could never hear enough to make the pain stop.

Haylee was drowning, and I watched from the shore, without a ring.

Chapter Seventeen

My feet pounded down the sidewalk. Home was only a short run away. And when I got there, what would I do? Hide the journal. Pretend I'd never been there. Pretend I'd never seen.

But Nick would tell, wouldn't he? He'd have to tell the police I'd been there, and they'd come to my house, and they'd knock on my door, and they'd wake up my mom—

Footsteps pounded behind me.

"Kira!" Nick called. "Wait up."

I slowed, my shoes still slamming into the sidewalk for several more steps. Then I felt Nick's hand on my shoulder. He spun me around to face him.

"Where are you going?" he said.

We were both panting, from the running, from the smoke, from finding the body. And I looked down at Nick's hands, and found he'd already hung up the phone.

He wasn't supposed to do that. He'd told the operator he'd stay on.

"Just don't tell them I was here, okay?" I said. "Tell them you drove by, and you stopped, and you heard the car, and you found him. Don't tell them it was me. Don't tell them about the journal."

Nick's hand ran down my forearm, and then his fingers laced

through mine.

My heart pounded. Maybe he'd been trying to take the journal and grabbed the wrong hand.

Shut up, Kira, I thought. *A guy doesn't hold your hand on accident.*

He squeezed my hand. "You promised you were going to tell me what Haylee wrote. Remember?"

"You," I said. "I said I'd tell *you*. Not the police." I shook my head. Too hard.

Nick's fingers tightened around mine. "You're shaking," he said. "You're really that afraid of people reading what's in there?"

I took a deep breath, then nodded. "Everyone will believe her," I said.

Nick looked over his shoulder, back at the house. I couldn't hear sirens. Would they use sirens, if they were coming for someone who was dead?

"Okay," Nick said. "Okay. We don't have to stay."

"He's your uncle," I said. "You have to go back."

"He's dead. You're—" He took a deep breath. "Let's go. We can read the journal together."

"Now?" I asked.

"Now," he said. He pulled me toward his car, which was parked still farther down the street.

I had no room to argue with that.

We reached the car, and Nick opened my door for me. When I sat down, I squeezed the journal between my knees and put my head in my hands.

He closed my door, and then he climbed in on the driver's side and started the car.

I heard the sirens now, far off.

Nick pulled onto the road, and drove in the other direction. I felt like the car was barely crawling forward, but when I looked over at the speedometer, Nick was driving at the speed limit.

"Do you want to read it to me?" Nick asked. "Or just tell me what it says?"

Where should I begin? Should I prepare him first, or let him

169

read it for himself? I looked down at the smooth edge of the journal's spine.

"Not here," I said. "Can we go somewhere?"

"Like where?"

"I don't know." We couldn't go to my house, or his, without waking our families up. Besides, someone would call his mom eventually. The police would know it was him who called 911.

I looked at the clock. It was midnight already. Hopefully Mom hadn't woken up when I left, or she'd have the police after me. "We could go to a park."

Nick nodded. "There's one this way."

Of course there was—the one that I'd been to with Bradley, where we'd apparently had sex right there in the trees.

I didn't want to remind Nick about that. I thought it might occur to him that I'd want to go somewhere else, but in minutes, I could see the treetops of the arboretum in the yellow park lights.

"This okay?" Nick asked.

"Fine," I said, though the other F word was really the one I meant. I wondered how people would react if I said *that* every time they asked me how I was doing. Lately, it'd be closer to the truth.

"They'll be looking for you, won't they?" I asked. "The police?"

"Not here," Nick said. "I'll just tell them you got scared, and I took you away to calm you down."

That wasn't too far from the truth. But it was still a lie. Nick had just offered to lie to the police for me. I guessed I shouldn't be surprised. That was the sort of thing a protective big brother might do.

Nick pulled into the parking lot and flipped off first the car, then the lights. Fluorescents shone from the corners of the parking lot, flooding the journal in my lap with yellow light. I pulled it out from between my knees.

I should tell him, so he heard the story my way first. Not in Haylee's words. I couldn't let her convince him.

But the words stuck in my throat. I couldn't get them out.

Nick pulled out his penlight, his keys rattling in his hand.

We sat in silence for another moment. Nick was still waiting for me to decide what I wanted to do. The police had to have found Aaron by now. Or the paramedics. Or the firemen. They'd be looking for us—for the people who called.

"They might trace your phone," I said.

"I shut it off. If they call, they'll get voice mail."

I shut my eyes. I had to tell him. But my mouth wouldn't form the words. "Let's just read."

Nick leaned over my shoulder. His breath tickled my ear. I opened the book to the first page, which was covered in Haylee's loopy handwriting.

She hadn't dated the entry, but her scrawl looked even messier than normal. She wrote:

Behold, people of my native land
I wend my latest way:
I gaze upon the latest light of day
That I shall ever see;
Death, who lays all to rest, is leading me
To Aecheron's far strand.

That sounded like it came from one of Haylee's plays, but I couldn't place it.

"Do you want to read it out loud?" Nick asked.

The book shook in my hands, and I didn't trust my voice.

I flipped the pages, but none of the entries were dated.

I wanted to rip the book in half at the spine. Had she written any of this in the last days of her life? How would I ever know?

His hands ran up her thighs. She'd written the words in the very center of one page, leaving the facing page blank. *Now his hands are tied. He runs only with his eyes.*

My face flushed. I turned the book away from Nick, gripping it tightly.

"Hey," Nick said. "If you're not going to read, at least let me see."

"Wait," I said. "Give me a minute to find it." I read on.

She doesn't know what to be for him. Which her is she? Who will she be today?

The fragments went on for pages; all of them were like that. Just words strung together.

He wants her to forget. And she tries and she tries and she tries. She wants to bleed it out, but it sticks like fat to her veins.

I scanned through looking for names. Mine. Haylee's. Bradley's. But she'd strung together sentences full of pronouns like identical beads on a string. Who could ever tell what this meant?

I grit my teeth. No one would recognize me in this. No wonder Hazel had been clueless.

Haylee left us nothing.

"Hey," Nick said again, nudging me.

I flipped more pages. Haylee said she'd written about me. Had she only said that to bother me? Because this was gibberish. Haylee left a journal, but she didn't leave me any answers at all.

I slammed the book closed, tossing it away. The corner of it hit the windshield and it bounced off, landing on the dash. The journal was nothing. Haylee left me with nothing, only the promise of an answer that would never come.

Nick put his hand on my arm, but I scrambled for my seatbelt, shoved open the door, and staggered out of the car, tripping over my own feet. I launched myself to the path under the trees, not seeing where I was going, or even trying to look.

I didn't realize Nick was following me until he grabbed me by the shoulder, spinning me around, momentum crushing me into him. I didn't realize I was crying until I was sobbing against him, the zipper teeth of his hoodie digging into my cheek.

"Hey, it's okay," he said in my ear. "It's going to be okay."

I knew that he couldn't be sure of that, but I didn't pull away. As my sobbing slowed, Nick pulled back, brushing my hair out of my face. I looked into his eyes. I expected to get that feeling, the rush of knowing that he was about to kiss me. But he just kept looking at me, maintaining his distance.

My breath was all jagged from crying, and snot collected in my nose, and I didn't know what to do.

So I kissed him.

Nick's lips felt soft against mine, and my knees dissolved. Nick supported me, our arms tight around each other's shoulders. And since he moved so slow, and so carefully, it took me a second to be sure he was kissing me back.

But the moment after I felt his mouth move, Nick pulled away, pressing his forehead against mine. "I don't—" he said. "I can't—"

I closed my eyes, waiting for the words I knew were coming: *You're like a sister to me; it's like kissing my cousin.*

His voice was anguished. "I don't want to be the guy you use to get over Haylee."

My eyes popped open. "No!" I said. "It's not like that. Not with you."

His eyes searched mine. "Are you sure?"

"Yes," I said. "Yes, yes."

His arms shifted downward, and his hands curled around my waist. "The timing is suspicious. Especially with . . . what we found."

Ugh. There were enough bodies between us to open a morgue. His arms remained around me, so close I could feel his heart beating in tandem with mine.

"Seriously," I said. "Screw the timing."

Nick kissed me like a man drowning in the ocean, who'd only now fought to the surface for air. This time, I had no problem figuring out what to do with my hands. Our bodies locked together, his arms pulling me tight against him, my elbows resting on his shoulders, my fingers in his hair. The kiss deepened, and I barely felt the cold night air around us. The world blurred, like we were the only two people in it, but somehow, this thought cut through: this guy had *never* thought of me as his sister.

When we broke apart, I curled against Nick's body, my forehead pressing against his neck. I wasn't the only one out of breath.

I lifted my chin and kissed him gently on the collar bone, right under the ribbed neck of his T-shirt.

Nick moaned softly. His lips pressed against my ear. "We should have done this years ago."

"You mean when I was twelve?" Gah. Nice, Kira. Remind him.

But Nick didn't seem phased. "That's when I first felt this way," he said. "I should have told you, then."

My twelve-year-old self wished he had. The me-now knew this was better. Still. I leaned back, looking into his eyes. "Why didn't you?" I asked. "In three years?"

And Nick Harbourne, his face deadpan, actually said these words to me: "I never thought you were interested."

The laugh burst out of me before I could stop it. I dissolved against him, a giggling, sniffling, gasping mess. In all the times I'd imagined kissing Nick, I'd never pictured it like this. But his arms stayed firm around me. We twisted together in one smooth motion, Nick turning me around and guiding me to the ground, so we sat on the sidewalk, my back tight against his chest.

"I've always liked you," I said. "Always."

He leaned forward, his chin on my shoulder, his nose brushing my ear. "But Haylee said . . ."

The earth seemed to sink out from underneath me, and I clung to Nick's arms. I already knew how that sentence would end, but I needed to hear it.

"What did she say?" I asked.

He sighed. "She said you were way too good for me. She said we were practically related. She called me a . . ."

"A what?"

"A perv."

I closed my eyes, tasting the betrayal.

Nick swore. "If you liked me, she must have known."

"She knew," I said. "She always knew." All the times she'd shrugged when I asked if Nick liked me. "And she knew you liked me back."

He nodded, resting his forehead on my shoulder. And we were both quiet.

Haylee had been keeping us apart.

"She was scared," Nick said finally. "She thought if we were together she'd be the third wheel, and she'd lose us both."

"Does that make it cut less?" I asked.

"No," Nick said. "But I wish it did. I don't want to be mad at her now."

That was the trouble with anger toward a ghost. There was no one to yell at.

Nick slid his palm under my chin, guiding my mouth back to his. This time his lips were hungrier. His tongue brushed gently against mine. I lifted myself onto his lap and turned into him. Our fingers laced together.

When we pulled apart, Nick pressed his forehead to mine. "This is better."

"Lots better," I said.

"And you don't think of me as family."

I laughed. "Definitely not." Even my mom seemed to like Nick. Though she wouldn't when she discovered where we'd been. I leaned back. "We need to get going," I said.

Nick groaned. "Do we?"

I wrapped my arms around him and leaned into his shoulder, squeezing him tight. "Tell me you won't regret this tomorrow," I said.

"I regret the last few years," he said. "But not this."

"It's not your fault," I said. "Haylee—"

"No," Nick said. "This is on me. I didn't have to let her scare me. I didn't have to listen."

I nodded. I didn't, either.

Nick helped me to my feet, and I sniffled. Nick reached into his pocket and pulled out a piece of white cloth, handing it to me.

"What on earth is that?" I asked.

"It's a handkerchief."

"Well, yeah. What are you, eighty-five?"

We both smiled. I took his handkerchief and wiped my face, and then stuffed it into my pocket. I'd wash it before giving it back.

And then Nick pulled something out of his jacket pocket and held it up to me.

The journal.

"Are you ready to deal with this?" he asked. "Because you don't have to if you don't want to."

I sniffled. "There's nothing in it," I said. "It's nonsense."

Nick pulled out his penlight and motioned to the side of the path. "Can I look?"

I nodded. "Sure."

Nick led me over to the same low wall I'd sat on with Bradley, but this time I wanted to be there. Nick wrapped one arm around me so the journal spread open in front of both of us. I liked the way I fit under his arm, the barrier between us broken for good.

Nick's penlight flipped over the loopy writing, and I followed the words.

And after a few pages, I started to pick out the pattern.

He says he's sorry, Haylee wrote. *But the plate, once broken, will never be whole again.*

And then later: *If she can't forget, she'll be alone. She speaks, but there's no one to hear. She flails, but there's no one who sees.*

Nick flipped pages, reading faster and faster, as if he just wanted to be done, but couldn't stop until he got to the end.

But he turned all her Raggedy Anns into Barbies. Show me where he touched you on the doll. But it's the wrong doll all together. It's not the right doll at all.

And the pieces of the puzzle floating in my mind snapped together as if drawn by magnets. It wasn't a code, but it wasn't gibberish, either.

A horrible sick feeling settled into my gut. "It wasn't me," I said.

Nick stopped reading. "What?"

"Haylee accused me of the things that happened to her." The

words were out of my mouth before I realized fully what they meant. I stopped, the rest of the thought hanging in the air, waiting for me to finish.

It was clear to me now. The words in the journal were thoughts Haylee had as she tried to process what was wrong with her. She left out the proper nouns because she couldn't bear to write them down, the way I couldn't tell Nick my whole story in coherent sentences.

"What did Haylee accuse you of?" Nick asked.

"She said she wrote that Aaron . . ." I couldn't say this. My lungs wouldn't draw air.

Nick tightened his arm around me. "If it's not true, it can't hurt you."

My heartbeat seemed to slow. I counted five arduous beats, and then sucked in a slow breath, all the way down to my toes. The words came out in a rush. I didn't dare pause between them, for fear I wouldn't be able to finish. "ShesaidAaronwasinterested inme."

Nick pulled back, trying to look me in the eye, but I turned away, pressing my cheek against his chest. I sniffled again.

"Interested in you," he said.

I wilted against him. "You know," I said. "Like . . . sexually."

Nick pulled away a strand of hair that had glued itself to my wet face. "But nothing ever happened."

"Nothing!" I said. "I mean, not to me."

Nick drew a deep breath. And I wished that the cold breeze would blow away the things we were going to say next, so I'd never have to hear them.

"You think that Aaron abused Haylee," Nick said.

I did. It was a horrible, twisted thought, but I thought it all the same. And my face burned as I thought about everything that meant. Everything that could have happened to me, even though it didn't.

"Tell me I'm wrong," I said. "Tell me I'm imagining it. Tell me Haylee was writing about something else."

"Actually," Nick said, "it makes a lot of things make sense."

My head spun, and I clung to Nick's side so I wouldn't sway right off the wall. "It does?" I asked.

Nick nodded, his eyebrows knitting together. "My mother wouldn't let my sister go to Haylee's house alone," he said. "She's ten—old enough to ride her bike over like we did. But she's not allowed to go unless we go with her."

"She's a lot younger," I said. "She wouldn't have much reason to visit Haylee alone."

"But that's true of all of our cousins," Nick said. "And once, I heard my mother say . . ."

His mother. She was Haylee's aunt. If she knew, she could have done something. "Do you think—"

"She knew," Nick said. "I think she knew."

But if she did, she would have done something. She would have saved her. Wouldn't she?

I was her best friend. *I* should have known. "If she knew, then Hazel knew." And if anyone should have protected Haylee, it was her own mother.

Nick seemed to deflate, his weight bearing down on me. We clung heavily to each other. And I let myself dwell on this one thought: Hazel knew, and she still encouraged Aaron to coach me. The road trips, the tournaments, the hours alone in the yard.

She knew, and she let it all happen. She knew, and she stayed.

"The divorce papers," I said. "This is why Hazel was filing for divorce."

"If it's true," Nick said, "she should have done that before."

Long before.

Why *didn't* she?

I thought of Haylee, her voice cold as ice, as she told me what her father wanted to do to me. How many years had she lived in the house with her own abuser? How many years had she lived with that fear?

"They sent her to a doctor, like she was the one who needed fixing," I said. "But it wasn't her. It was *him*."

The leaves rustled in the trees above us. Nick shut the journal and pocketed his light. And we spent several minutes in silence.

"What do we do?" I said finally.

"What do you mean?" Nick asked.

"There has to be some justice for her."

"She's dead," he said. "He's dead. What kind of justice can there be?"

If Hazel knew, and she did nothing, *she* should pay.

"Come on," Nick said, standing off the wall and pulling me up by my hands. "Let's go home. We can get some sleep, and figure things out in the morning."

I couldn't imagine that things would make more sense then than they did now, but I followed Nick anyway. We walked slowly back to the car, like neither of us wanted to reach it. Nick held my hand, tight like I might slip away. And I squeezed back, so he'd know that I had no intention of letting go.

We rounded the bend, leaving the arboretum behind, but when the parking lot came into view, I stopped short.

There, on the far end of the lot, a car had parked in the shadow beneath a draping eucalyptus tree.

A car that belonged to Bradley Johansen.

Nine Days Before

Haylee always forced me to proofread her English essays. I wasn't any good at it, but it kept me informed about what I was supposed to have read.

Haylee dragged her *Tess* essay over to my house after school, and braided my hair in fishtails while I read it.

In the end, Haylee wrote, *Tess kills Alec, but she can't kill the part of herself that she hates. I guess once someone damages you in that way, there isn't any way to get better.*

"You and your tragedy," I said. "Maybe if you liked them less, you wouldn't have to live like you were in one."

"Maybe I like them because I *am* in one," Haylee said.

I turned back to the essay.

Angel is Tess's savior, she wrote. *He is her ideal man, the one she can dream and hope about and love. But when he betrays her, all is lost. Without that ideal to fall back on, she loses the light of hope in her life. She has nothing left but despair.*

"So what's the moral of the story?" I asked. "Don't love anybody? Don't put people on pedestals?"

"There is no moral," Haylee said. "It's just sad."

I threw the essay over my shoulder at her. "What is the point of that?"

But Haylee just shook her head at me, her hands poised over my head mid-braid. "The fact that you don't know," she said to me, "is proof you'll get a happy ending."

"I don't live in a comedy," I said.

Haylee shrugged. "You don't live in a tragedy, either."

Chapter Eighteen

Nick tried to pull me toward his car, but I planted my feet. He held my hand, our arms stretched between us as I stared at Bradley's car. The lights were out, but I knew why Bradley parked here. I knew what sorts of things he'd be doing.

Like the turning of an ignition, this thought roared to life: it wasn't just Aaron's fault that Haylee was dead. It was also Bradley's. He'd pushed her over the edge—made her lose hope in her future. Maybe he'd slept with her and discarded her. Maybe that was enough.

Or maybe he'd raped her. Haylee wasn't here to tell me which, but I didn't care.

He had to face what he did, either way.

I twisted out of Nick's grip and ran across the parking lot. My hands reached for my pocket. I was going to key his car. I was going to puncture his tires. There would be nothing left of his windows.

I was ten feet away when I saw the back of Bradley's greasy head lift over the back seat.

I stopped. I stood at Bradley's bumper, just under the branches of the tree, watching as Bradley flung a white bra up into the back window. Catherine sat up, her mouth meeting his, only her head and neck visible over the back of the seat. She had her hair pulled back in a simple braid. And though I knew it had to be a trick of the light, for a split second, her profile looked like Haylee.

I stepped around the car, jerked open the door, grabbed Bradley by his shoulders, and hauled him out of the car. Even as his ass hit the concrete, he reached to zip up his fly. In the back seat, Catherine shrieked and wrapped her hands over her chest.

Nick grabbed me from behind. I shrugged him off. Nick was shouting something, and Catherine was screaming at me, but the only one I was focused on was Bradley.

"You're not going to get away with what you did to her," I said.

Bradley rolled to his feet and backed up against the car. "Crazy bitch," he shouted at me. "We broke up. Get over it."

My hands itched for something to throw at him. "Get over it? I was never *into* it. But I know what you did to Haylee, and soon everyone else will, too."

Everyone fell silent. I could feel Nick's hands at my elbows, trying to pull me away, but I held firm. Huddled in the backseat, Catherine scrambled back into her shirt.

"Please," Bradley said. "She was dying to have me."

Bad choice of words. Nick let go of me and stepped up to Bradley. "Shut up," he said.

"Oh, come on, Harbourne," Bradley said. "I saw you pick her up from that party last summer. What was it, three AM? Four?"

"Five-thirty," Nick said. His voice was so small, I almost didn't hear him. I grabbed his wrist, but he wouldn't meet my eyes.

"She couldn't even walk straight," Bradley said. "She threw up on the way to your car, *and* in it."

"She just needed a ride," Nick said.

"And she didn't get one from the guy who just got done with her. Wonder why? Oh, right. Because she didn't even know his name."

Nick spoke through his teeth. "Shut. *Up.*"

Haylee never said anything to me about Nick picking her up from parties. Nick never said anything, either.

I turned away from Nick, and stepped up into Bradley's face instead. "It doesn't matter what else Haylee did. You forced yourself on her. You *killed* her."

Bradley looked me right in the eye. His breath smelled of spearmint gum. "I didn't do anything she wasn't begging me to do."

I caught him by the throat, just under his jaw. His eyes widened in surprise as I forced his head back into the roof of his car. For a moment I felt stronger than him. Superior. And then he socked me in the stomach so hard that I staggered back.

Nick was on him so fast that I didn't see him coming. Judging by his reaction, Bradley hadn't, either. Nick pinned Bradley to the car with both arms; Nick's knees kept Bradley from using his legs. Bradley clawed at Nick, arching his back away from the car, trying to find leverage. Catherine—shirt restored—scrambled out of the car and shoved Nick in the shoulder, trying to get him off.

I pushed Catherine back into the car. She didn't put up much of a fight, but as she sat down on the seat, she shot me a hateful glance. "What the hell are you doing here?" she asked.

I opened my mouth to answer, but out of the corner of my eye, I caught sight of my glove, still on the floor of Bradley's car. I pushed Catherine aside and grabbed it, when bright beams of light shot through the windows of Bradley's car, and flashed in blazes of red and white.

A bullhorn sounded. "Hands up. Step away from the car." I put my hands in the air, though one of them still had the glove. Bradley and Nick both faced the oncoming cop car with their arms sticking up in the air, while Catherine cowered on the backseat like she wanted to disappear.

A few days ago, I would have felt like that, too.

But now, all I wanted was to be seen.

Ten Hours After

On a Monday in the middle of December, I was in the bathroom brushing my teeth before school when I heard Mom's cell phone ring. Mom always dropped me off on her way to work at the middle school, but sometimes she'd be needed in her office early in the morning, and then she'd rush me out the door and strand me on campus while she ran off to her meeting.

Sure enough, Mom knocked on my door while I was stuffing my geometry book into my backpack, homework papers sticking out the side. A corner of one of the papers caught on the zipper and tore.

"I'm almost ready," I called. "Can you take me to Haylee's so I don't have to be at school so early?"

Mom opened the door a crack.

"Kira?" she said.

Mom's tone was heavy, like she'd just been handed a heavy weight. I froze with my book still hanging out of the zipper. What had I done to make trouble? I hadn't skipped class. I was passing all my classes, as far as I knew. "Hazel won't mind," I said. "She has to drive to school anyway."

Mom pushed the door open farther. Her face was blanched. "Kira," she said. "Can you sit down for a minute?"

Some people say that they know about bad things right before they happen. They get prickles on their neck, and their hair stands on end, and they just *know*.

But I just stood there, trying to figure out what I'd done.

And then Mom said, "It's Haylee."

"On the phone?" I asked. I checked my phone in my pocket. It was on. She'd have called me before she called Mom, though I'd called her a dozen times—more—over the weekend, and she hadn't answered.

Mom shook her head. "Her parents found her this morning in her room. She's dead, honey. She killed herself last night."

I want to say that house tilted or the room spun, or the floor exploded out from under me—a bang to separate this new way of being from the old. But the truth is, everything just grew very, very still, like the air was thinner, and sound didn't carry. I looked at a spot on my carpet where I'd spilled a cup of Kool-aid six months ago. The carpet was dyed pink there. It would never be white again.

"Kira?" Mom said.

"How can you say that?" I asked.

Mom pressed her fingers to her lips before she answered. "Because it's true," she said. "I'm so sorry."

"No," I said. "I mean how can you *say* that, like, like . . ."

Like it's real.

"I didn't want you to hear it at school," Mom said. She was trying to answer my question, even though it didn't make sense.

I pulled out my phone. "I'll just call her," I said. She'd ignored my texts all weekend, just like my calls. But if I texted her now, surely she'd answer. And Mom would be wrong. And it would all be a mistake.

"You can't call her," Mom said slowly. "She's gone."

So what would happen? No one would answer? Because Haylee ignored my calls all the time. That didn't mean she was dead.

"Kira?" Mom asked. "I think you should stay home from school today."

"Yeah," I said. "Okay." Because the world was falling ever more silent. Mom's voice faded away, like someone turned the volume knob on the world.

If I couldn't hear anything, then I wouldn't be able to hear those words. *She's dead. She's gone. She. Killed. Herself.*

Afterward, I would try to figure out what it was Mom *should* have said. I would reword the sentences over and over, trying to make them sound nice. Gentle. Comforting. Mom must have done that, too. She must have agonized over each word with every step up the stairs. She was a psychologist. She should have known what to say.

Finally, what I decided was this: the words "dead" and "Haylee" didn't belong in the same sentence. There was no right way to say it. Ever.

And now, they'd always be paired.

Chapter Nineteen

The driver's side door of the police car opened, and the silhouette of an officer stepped out—a woman barely taller than me.

And before she could say anything else, I pointed at Bradley and shouted at her. "He raped Haylee Ricks," I said. "He's the reason she killed herself."

And Bradley yelled over me, his voice louder than mine, "She's a stalker. She attacked us! I want to file assault charges."

Assault charges? Oh no. I *had* shoved him. And tossed him out of the car. And grabbed him by the throat. I had no proof of what he'd done to Haylee. Even the journal wouldn't help. It'd be my word against his.

The officer hesitated, backlit by the headlights.

"He attacked *me*," I yelled. "Last week. In the woods right over there."

Bradley turned toward me, and Nick stepped between us before I could see the look on his face.

"Put your hands on the car, all of you," the officer said. As I did, I realized every inch of my body was shaking.

Nick gave me a wide eyed look as the officer hauled Catherine from the car, and searched us all. Bradley tried to chatter excuses at her, but she held up her hand and barked at him to shut up.

This time, Bradley did.

When she searched Nick, she took the journal from him and flipped it open.

"It's Haylee's," Nick said. "She killed herself before Christmas. It's evidence."

As the officer carried it to her car, Bradley watched her go with wide eyes, and then turned a hateful stare at me. I smiled what I hoped was a knowing smile. Maybe he believed me about what Haylee wrote in the journal.

The officer stuffed Bradley and Catherine into the back of the cop car and locked them there, while Nick and I still stood with our hands on Bradley's car.

"Sorry," I whispered to Nick. I'd dragged him into all this.

"Don't be," Nick said.

"Are you kidding? We're in so much trouble."

"Yeah," Nick said. "But you're worth it."

I about melted into the car. I was worth it? All this? Too bad once Mom got a hold of me, I wouldn't see him again until I was thirty.

A second car pulled into the parking lot, and I hunched down. But it wasn't my mother, just another police officer, coming to haul Nick and me in. Together we climbed into the back seat. As the officer shut us in, I reached for Nick's hand. He met me halfway.

But as we drove in, my heartbeat refused to slow. I knew what I had to do. "I'm going to tell them everything," I said to Nick.

"Everything?" he asked.

"Everything." From Bradley, to the break in, to the lies Haylee told. They'd piece together a lot of it anyway, but that wasn't enough. It had to be said. *I* had to say it. I was never going to get a better chance than this one.

"Okay," Nick said. "But if my parents don't let me out of the house until I graduate from college, don't say I didn't warn you."

I squeezed his hand. If I didn't tell now, he'd never see me again, anyway. I would disappear. I would entirely cease to be.

Nick's mom showed up at the station before mine did. Mom hadn't said much over the phone when I called her. I was pretty sure she'd hung up the phone before fully understanding my words.

Nick's mom, on the other hand, chewed him out on her cell phone half the way to the station, until he finally told her he had to hang up.

She marched into the station wearing jeans and a stained T-shirt she might have been sleeping in, her hair a frizzy mess around her face.

She opened her mouth to yell at him again, but Nick spoke first.

"You knew," he said, looking her in the eyes. "You knew all along what Uncle Aaron did to Haylee."

He could have said that over the phone, but he hadn't. He'd waited until now, when he could look her in the eyes. And Nick's mom didn't have to say anything. The sad, stricken look on her face said it all.

Nick shook his head, like he didn't quite know what to say to that.

But I did. "Someone should have saved her. Before it was too late."

Nick's mom sank into a chair across from us. "She was six," she said. Her voice was small, just as Nick's had been earlier, when he admitted to picking Haylee up from that party.

"What?" I asked.

She sighed. "Haylee was six when Aaron abused her. When Hazel told me, I said she should leave him. But he willingly went to counseling—they all did. And Hazel thought they could fix it. She thought it could all be okay."

Nick's face turned gray. "They split up. Aaron and Hazel—that year when I was eight."

His mom nodded. "He wasn't allowed to come back until the therapist cleared him."

"She was *six*?" I said. "That was so long ago."

Nick's mom shrugged. "Some wounds go deep enough that they don't heal."

I leaned back in my seat. Judging by what happened, this one must have festered. "But he should have gone to jail," I said. I knew the rules my mom had to work under. She wasn't allowed to keep secrets about abuse. "The therapist should have filed a report."

"There was a report," Nick's mom said. "But he got help. Hazel didn't want to press charges, and the state decided not to carry it to court."

My mouth fell open. They'd failed her. Even her own family wouldn't protect her.

We all sat there, watching each other in silence, until an officer came to lead us to two different rooms—one for Nick and his mom, and one for me. Bradley sat alone in a room at the end of the hall. He looked up at the ceiling, as if going over his story in his head.

For my sake, I hoped it wasn't a good one.

When the officer led me to my room, I sat down in the chair by the table. "I want to wait for my mother," I said.

The officer nodded and shut the door.

I was only going to tell this story once.

The officer escorted Mom back after what seemed like an eternity. She was wearing sweats and a heavy jacket, even though I knew it wasn't that cold out. Her face was still wrinkled from her pillow.

"Don't yell," I said to her. "I'm going to explain everything."

"I don't see how you could possibly—"

"Please!" I yelled. "Please just sit down and let me talk?"

Mom looked like her head was going explode, but she sat.

I looked up at the officer. "I need to tell you everything," I said. "Everything about Haylee Ricks."

I wished I could go back and do things differently. To really hear what Haylee was saying—the things I never understood. But I couldn't. Not ever.

It was too late to save Haylee. But it wasn't too late to break her silence.

It wasn't too late to speak the words she couldn't say.

191

Eight Years Before

In second grade, Haylee wore a dress to school every day. They were always light and gauzy, with layered skirts that hung from her frame like wings. Other girls showed up in shorts and T-shirts, hoodies and jeans, but not Haylee. She floated through school, with her hair braided around her head in a wreath.

"I can't believe her mother dresses her like that," Mom said one day as she dropped me off.

But secretly, I wished mine would.

Maybe from jealousy, maybe from seven-year-old spite, Kendra Thompson called her names, turned away from her at lunch, talked to Maxine Ferrera about birthday parties that Haylee wasn't invited to. But Haylee didn't change.

One day she climbed up on the playground equipment with an armful of clover from the yard. She stood on a raised platform next to the monkey bars, tucking the flowers into the folds of her hair. Two boys from an older grade stood directly under her, snickering and shoving each other out of the way to look up her dress.

I climbed the ladder beside her, and pointed down at them. When Haylee looked down, her eyes widened.

Then I swung across the monkey bars, kicking forward as hard as I could, and knocked one of them in the head on the backswing.

"Hey!" he shouted, and chased after me. But I pulled myself up the monkey bars and perched on top, out of his reach.

"She kicked me in the head!" the kid roared at the yard duty.

"It was an accident," Haylee said. "He was standing under there where no one could see him."

"Get down from there," the yard duty said to me.

And she looked at the kid under the play set and Haylee standing over him in her dress, and she hauled the boys to the other side of the yard to talk to them.

"Thanks," Haylee said, tucking another clover into her braids.

"I like your hair," I said.

Haylee's smile brightened. "Can I do yours?"

And I swung down off the bars and sat on a bench with the sun shining in my eyes while Haylee braided my long hair into a crown that matched hers.

"I thought your mom did your hair," I said.

"Nope," Haylee said. "I do it myself."

"Will you do mine tomorrow?" I asked.

"Every day, if you want," Haylee said.

When she finished the braided crown, she pulled the clovers from her own hair and tucked them into mine.

"Look at Princess Kira," Kendra said. "She's joined the fairy club."

But Maxine must have missed the sarcasm in Kendra's voice, because she came over to sit next to me on the bench.

"Can I be next?" she asked Haylee.

And Haylee did Maxine's hair up in a twist, with her curls hanging out the back like a tassel.

"Don't worry," Haylee whispered to me as Maxine flounced away. "I did yours the best."

And from that day on, Haylee always gave me the best she had. But some days, sometimes, all she had to give was a deep well of darkness.

It was on those days that I loved her the most.

Chapter Twenty

I got a ticket for breaking curfew, but that was nothing com-
pared to the clinginess of my mother. It took a few days before
Mom would let me leave the house for anything except for
school. She hovered over me like a mother hen, making me
breakfast, sitting across from me at the table and asking me to
talk.

And so I did. I told her about the things Haylee used to say
to me, about the parties I knew she went to, about the times
she talked about making her exit.

"I should have told you this stuff before," I said, picking apart
a bagel. "Maybe you could have helped her."

"Maybe," Mom said. "Or maybe I could have helped *you*."

I rolled a bit of bagel between my fingers until it squished as
soft as dough. I knew she was right.

I floated through school, as if encapsulated in an invisible
bubble. I heard the whispers and the lectures, but they all
seemed distant. Each day, though, the protective layer grew
thinner, and the outside world grew closer. Someday soon it
was going to disappear entirely. The world would get in, and
I'd have to feel it fully.

I was almost ready.

Catherine avoided me, though I was pretty sure that was
mostly out of embarrassment, because I heard from one of the

girls on our softball team that she'd been telling everyone what a monster Bradley was.

Bradley hadn't shown up at school. He was still saying that he and Haylee had consensual sex. And maybe they did. Haylee had idolized him for so long. He was her Angel, her last hold-out hope for love, just like Tess. Maybe the disappointment of seeing him up close was enough to send her over the edge.

But I'd seen the real Bradley when we were alone in the trees. Whatever happened, he had a hand in it.

Without Haylee to give us the details, there were no criminal charges, but accusations were enough to get him suspended from school sports pending investigation.

Word was, his parents were looking into private schools. Good riddance.

I spent lunches by the portables with Nick. Sometimes we talked and sometimes we didn't, but as the barrier between me and the rest of the world grew thinner, I could feel the bond between us growing stronger.

There was no funeral for Aaron, just a private, family burial. Nick was invited. His mom went, but he didn't. "I'll just be angry," he told me. "I don't want to be angry at anyone's funeral."

And I didn't try to change his mind. Instead, I held his hand.

The first weekend after the incident at the park, there was a knock on our door early in the morning. I was sitting in the kitchen, pouring myself juice, and I made it to the door before Mom did.

When I opened it, Hazel stood on our front steps. She looked up at me, her face gray. Sharp lines crossed her forehead and cheeks. I could swear they hadn't been there before.

Before either of us spoke, I heard footsteps behind me. "What are you doing here?" Mom asked. Her voice was cold.

"I'm sorry," Hazel said. "I'll go. I just came to bring you this." She pulled something out of her pocket. A package, wrapped in old newsprint.

A present from Haylee.

"She wrapped it before," Hazel said. "I put it in the closet with the others, because I didn't know what to do with it. But I thought . . . I thought you might want it."

I took it from her. "Thank you," I said.

I could feel Mom behind me, looming. I knew there were things she wanted to say, about how Hazel had endangered me, how Hazel not only failed to protect her own daughter, but sheltered a man who could have abused me, too.

But as I looked Hazel in the eye, I realized I didn't want Mom to say it. Hazel lost her daughter, and her husband, both in the same house. She'd been trying to save them, in her way. Now she had to live with her failure, just like I did. Only she knew the truth all along. She'd always know there was more she should have done.

Nothing Mom or I could say would be worse than living with that.

"Can I ask you a question?" I asked.

Hazel's lips pressed into a thin line. "Yes," she said.

I spoke slowly, softly, like I was coaxing a frightened animal. "Did it really just happen when Haylee was six?"

Tears welled up in Hazel's red-rimmed eyes. "Yes," she said. "That's what Haylee told her therapist."

"Then why?" I asked. "Why kill himself now?"

She wiped her eyes with the back of her hand. "He thought Haylee would get better," she said. "We both did."

And now there was no hope of that. And therefore no hope for him. Their failure was devastating.

"Why didn't you leave him?" I asked. She knew I'd been in her house. There were no secrets now. "Why not file the divorce papers until now?"

Hazel's voice shook as she answered. "I just," she said, "I just wanted everything to be fine."

She looked at me, and I saw the wide pit gaping open before her. I wanted to say something to keep it from swallowing her whole, but I couldn't.

There was nothing I could do to save her from the consequences of her silence.

She turned to go, and I stood in the doorway, watching her get into her car and drive away.

"That was kind of you," Mom said, "not to tell her what a monster she is." I heard the part Mom didn't say: *kinder than I would have been.*

I leaned against the doorway. "I don't want to hurt her. There's enough of that going around." And as I walked up to my room with the package, I realized I meant what I said.

I sat on my bed and lifted the tape. I shook the package, and a framed photo slid out onto my bed.

Two faces grinned up at me—Haylee's and mine. It was a dressing-room photo from the day we went shopping for Winter Fling dresses for Haylee's date with Bradley. Haylee must have printed and wrapped it that same day. I had on this totally ridiculous lime green prom dress with a pink flounce—a dress that made me look huge and hideous and which I would never pay money for in a million years. Haylee was wearing a low-cut silver number that really showed off her curves.

Soon after, she'd be wearing a coffin. And she didn't even leave me a note to say goodbye.

And that's when I knew, even before I looked. I flipped the frame over and slid out the cardboard backing.

There, on the back of the photo, was Haylee's loopy handwriting. She'd written our names and the date—the same day we went shopping. And below that I found the two most important sentences in the world. *Kira, I love you*, she'd written. *You are the very best friend in the world.* Tears welled up in my eyes, mostly because I knew it wasn't true. The best friend would have saved her. The best friend would have seen what I couldn't, and known what to do about it.

But Haylee loved the friend that she had. At least I got to hear that piece of the truth from her.

The next day was Sunday, and Mom agreed to let me go to the cemetery with Nick. We parked at the entrance and walked the long paths to her grave, my hand in his.

197

Haylee's spot was still unmarked. I'd come to the graveyard to find Haylee's ghost, but as we sat down in the grass at the foot of her grave, I knew she wasn't here. There was nothing here but dirt and stones, and a body she'd left behind. I thought I'd accepted that she wasn't coming back. How long would it take me to stop looking everywhere for her?

I picked a clover and rolled it between my fingers. I plucked another, then another. I hadn't made clover chains in years, but my fingers remembered how. Haylee and I had made hundreds of them, maybe thousands. In elementary school, the most tragic day of the week was Wednesday, after the grass was mowed, when we'd find all our flowers cut to pieces. But it only took them a few days to grow back.

"You didn't bring her any flowers," I said.

"Not today," Nick said. "We can bring some tomorrow."

"It's okay," I said. "She only liked flowers because she wanted to wear them in her hair."

I couldn't braid my hair as well as Haylee could. But I pulled a tendril away from my face and braided my clover chain into it, the white flowers shedding their tiny bladed petals onto my shoulders as I went. When I reached the back I secured it with an elastic, and then started up the other side so the two braids would meet at the back.

When I finished, Nick brushed wild hairs from my face, tucking them behind my ear. Haylee wouldn't have left strands loose like that. Her braids would be perfectly smooth. And though it's a stupid thing, it's one of a million that are gone from the world along with Haylee. My shoulders bowed under the weight of that.

Haylee was gone. And a part of me would always be sad about that.

But now, as Nick leaned in to kiss me, there was no rush of panic or of need, just the quiet, slow brushing of the breeze against my skin.

I kept my eyes open. I wanted to see.

Acknowledgments

I wrote the first draft of this novel in 2004. Over the intervening ten years, it went through many different drafts. Because of the length of the process, it's impossible for me to thank everyone who critiqued this book by name. If I forget you, forgive me, and know that I appreciate your feedback, and your support. Thank you, thank you.

The first and most important thanks go to Kristy Kugler and Melody Fender. Kristy and Melody have not only been among my best friends, they have also been my loyal cheerleaders. Without Kristy's fabulous editing, this book would be much worse than it is—and indeed, would likely not exist. I feel truly honored to have a cover designed by Melody, who has always had a knack for making things beautiful. I love you girls. Thanks for believing in me.

Also Isaac Stewart—layout master, design guru—thank you for lending me your expertise. Without it, I would not have dared to attempt this book on my own. To Michelle Argyle and Sandra Tayler, thanks for all the advice about self-publishing, and for paving the way. Your courage is an example to many, most of all me.

Thank you to my agent, the incomparable Eddie Schneider, for his tireless work on this book, and on all my books. Seriously,

Eddie. You do so much more than I could reasonably expect. Thank you.

Alaya Dawn Johnson read this book in one of its later forms, and gave some razor sharp feedback that allowed me to envision it as the book it is now. Thank you, Alaya. Without your feedback, this book would have forever remained an unsolvable problem. Your criticism was priceless. I am in your debt.

Thanks to all my writing groups, who have endured varying stages of drafts that eventually became this book. They are (in chronological order): The Publings, that Leading Edge aftercrowd, the Mistborn Llamas, the Rats with Swords, the Seizure Ninjas, Chris Crowe's 521 class, the Hermaphroditic Nazi Tarantuadogs, the Skype crowd, and the Johnny Hollis School of Illegal Teenage Driving. Working with all of you has been my pleasure. Thank you for the fine insights over the years.

There were a number of writing classes in both my undergraduate and graduate years who also read parts of this book. Thanks both to my professors, and my classmates, for the good times and good feedback. Also my beta readers: I dare not try to name you all, for I will forget too many of you. Thank you; you all rock. Special thanks to beta readers Tara Creel and Kathy Cowley, who read more recent drafts and gave great notes.

The fine people at the Utah Arts Council awarded this book first place in the category of young adult novel, back in the days when the book was called *Haylee's Journal*. Thanks to the Utah Arts Council for the ray of encouragement in the sea of rejection. Thanks especially to judge Todd Mitchell for his fine feedback, which gave me direction to give this book yet another revision.

And finally, my husband, Drew. You handle having a wife with her brain perpetually stuck in a book as if it's completely normal. (And for you, I guess it is!) You're always the first to tell me my work is good, and the first to tell me I can fix it when I discover it's not. I love you.

Janci Patterson is the author of two contemporary young adult novels: Everything's Fine, which won the Utah Arts Council award for Best Young Adult Novel in 2007, and Chasing the Skip, which was released by Christy Ottaviano books in 2012. For more about Janci, visit her online at jancipatterson.com.

CHASING
THE SKIP

JANCI PATTERSON

Ricki's dad has never been there for her. He's a bounty hunter who spends his time chasing parole evaders—also known as "skips"—all over the country. But now since Ricki's mom ran off, Ricki finds herself an unwilling passenger in a front-row seat to her father's dangerous lifestyle.

Ricki's feelings get even more confused when her dad starts chasing seventeen-year-old Ian Burnham. She finds herself unavoidably attracted to the dark-eyed felon who seems eager to get acquainted. But Ricki thinks she's ever in control—the perfect manipulator. Little does she know that Ian isn't playing their game by her rules.

www.ingramcontent.com/pod-product-compliance
Lightning Source LLC
Chambersburg PA
CBHW060438180626
46817CB00007B/2870